By royal decree, Harlequin Presents is delighted to
bring you THE ROYAL HOUSE OF NIROLI. Step into
the glamorous, enticing world of the Nirolian Royal
Family. As the king ails he must find an heir...each
month an exciting new installment follows the epic
search for the true Nirolian king. Eight heirs, eight
romances, eight fantastic stories! Favorite author
Penny Jordan starts this fabulous new series with
The Future King's Pregnant Mistress. It's time for
playboy Prince Marco Fierezza to claim his rightful
place—on the throne! But what will the king-in-waiting
do when he discovers his mistress is pregnant?

Plus, Lucy Monroe brings you the final part of her
MEDITERRANEAN BRIDES duet, *Taken: The Spaniard's
Virgin*, where Miguel takes Amber's innocence. There's
another sexy Spaniard in Trish Morey's *The Spaniard's
Blackmailed Bride*, when Blair is blackmailed into
marriage but Diablo's touch sets her body on fire!
In *Bought for the Greek's Bed* by Julia James,
Theo demands his new bride also be his wife in the
bedroom. In *The Greek Millionaire's Mistress* by
Catherine Spencer, Gina Hudson goes to settle an old
score in Athens, only to fall into the arms—and bed!—
of a tycoon. *The Sicilian's Red-Hot Revenge* by
Kate Walker has a handsome, fiery Italian who wants
revenge, but what happens when he discovers he's
going to be a father? In Annie West's *The Sheikh's
Ransomed Bride*, powerful Sheikh Rafiq rescues Belle
from rebels, only to demand marriage in return! And in
Maggie Cox's *The Millionaire Boss's Baby*, a brooding
boss's sensual seduction proves too good to resist.
Enjoy!

Bedded by... *Blackmail*
Forced to bed...then to wed?

He's got her firmly in his sights and she's got
only one chance of survival—surrender to his
blackmail...and him...in his bed!

Bedded by... Blackmail

The *big* miniseries from Harlequin Presents®

Dare you read it?

Trish Morey

THE SPANIARD'S BLACKMAILED BRIDE

Bedded by...

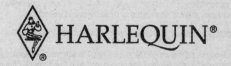

Blackmail

Forced to bed...then to wed?

HARLEQUIN®

TORONTO • NEW YORK • LONDON
AMSTERDAM • PARIS • SYDNEY • HAMBURG
STOCKHOLM • ATHENS • TOKYO • MILAN • MADRID
PRAGUE • WARSAW • BUDAPEST • AUCKLAND

ISBN-13: 978-0-373-12647-7
ISBN-10:   0-373-12647-6

THE SPANIARD'S BLACKMAILED BRIDE

First North American Publication 2007.

www.eHarlequin.com

Printed in U.S.A.

All about the author...
Trish Morey

TRISH MOREY wrote her first book at age eleven for a children's book-week competition: entitled *Island Dreamer,* it proved to be her first rejection. Shattered and broken, she turned to a life where she could combine her love of fiction with her need for creativity—and became a chartered accountant.☺ Life wasn't all dull though, as she embarked on a skydiving course, completing three jumps before deciding that she'd given her fear of heights a run for its money.

Meanwhile, she fell in love and married a handsome guy who cut computer code. After the birth of their second daughter, Trish spied an article saying that Harlequin® was actively seeking new authors. It was one of those eureka moments—Trish was going to be one of those authors!

Eleven years after reading that fateful article, the magical phone call came and Trish finally realized her dream. According to Trish, writing and selling a book is a major life achievement that ranks right up there with jumping out of an airplane and motherhood. All three take commitment, determination and sheer guts, but the effort is so very, very worthwhile.

Trish now lives with her husband and four young daughters in a special part of south Australia, surrounded by orchards and bushland and visited by the occasional koala and kangaroo.

You can visit Trish at her Web site at www.trishmorey.com or e-mail her at trish@trishmorey.com.

For Anne Gracie, who introduced me to Diablo.

One fantastic author.
An even better friend.

Thanks, Anne, this one's for you!

CHAPTER ONE

IT WAS much too late for a social call.

Briar Davenport crossed the entrance hall uneasily, the click of her heels on the dusty terrazzo tiles echoing in the lofty space while a premonition that all was not right in the world played havoc with her nerves.

Late-night visitors rarely meant good news.

The chimes rang out yet again and she reined in an unfamiliar urge to yell for whoever it was to hang on. But Davenports never yelled through doors—even when their senses were strained tight from trying to work out which family heirloom to send next to auction—it was bad enough that these days they were reduced to opening them.

Her hand hovered over the door handle for a moment while she took a deep breath, trying to calm her frayed nerves and think logically. It didn't *have* to be bad news. Sooner or later their run of bad luck had to change. Why not tonight?

Then she pulled open the door and bad luck just got worse.

'*You!*'

Diablo Barrentes leant into the open doorway, one arm propped high above her head, his black-clad torso arching over hers, and it was all she could do not to reel back from the sheer force of his hard-wired body. In the spill of the entry lighting he looked more like an extension of the night sky than a man—dark and filled with untold dangers. Tonight his shoulder-length black hair was pulled back into a short ponytail that did nothing to detract from his masculinity and everything to emphasize his dramatic buccaneer looks, but it was the flash of triumph in those black-lit eyes, the slight upturn at the corners of his full lips, that turned her thoughts to sudden panic and had her fingers itching to jam that piece of timber right back where it had come from.

Instead she forced herself to stand her ground, jagging her chin higher as if it might increase her already not insubstantial height. In heels her eyes fell but an inch short of his.

'What do you want?'

'I'm surprised,' he said, one side of his mouth rising higher as if amused by her efforts to match his height. 'I half expected you to slam the door in my face.'

Oh, Lord, the last thing she needed was to be reminded of how much her fingers itched to do just that. Already her grip on the door had turned her knuckles white as she schooled her voice to clipped civility. 'Then I don't need to tell you you're not welcome here.'

'Still, I am here.'

Four words, four simple words, and yet spoken in the remnants of that rich Castilian accent like a threat. Fear tracked a spidery path through her veins.

'Why?'

'And how delightful to see you too, *Briar*,' he said, ignoring her question while emphasizing her incivility. But being polite was hardly a concern to her right now. Not when his accent curled around her name as if he were devouring it.

As if he were devouring her.

She shivered. If he thought that, then he was definitely reading the wrong menu.

'Believe me,' she squeezed out, battling to keep her voice even, 'the pleasure is all yours.'

He laughed, barely more than a chuckle, a low sound that rumbled, somehow insinuating itself into her flesh and right through to her bones.

'*Sí,*' he agreed, his eyes making no apology as they traversed her length, all the way from her eyes, searing a trail over her curves and down her designer denim-clad legs to her pink leather boots, and then all the way up again.

The slow way.

The hot way.

His eyes, heavy with raw heat and firm possession, finally returned to hers and it was all she could do to remember to breathe.

'It's been my pleasure, indeed,' he murmured.

Anger bubbled to the surface with her very next intake of air, overtaking the slow sizzle his hooded gaze had left in its wake. How dared he look at her that way—as if he owned her? He had no right! Diablo Barrentes was kidding himself if he ever thought he would possess her. He'd never even come close.

Even so, she couldn't stop herself crossing her arms over her chest. If her nipples looked anywhere near as rock-hard as they felt, he would be in no doubt as to how that seemingly lazy once-over had affected her, and she didn't want him to know about it. She would rather not have to acknowledge that fact herself.

'You still haven't told me why you're here.'

'I've come to see your father.'

'I doubt it. I seriously doubt my father would ever want to see you again—not after everything you've done to undermine his business and ruin our lives in the process.'

He shrugged, lifting his thick dark eyebrows in a way that told her he didn't care what she thought, infuriating her even more.

'Your doubts are not my concern. My business, however, is, and right now you are preventing me from conducting that business. So, if you'll just move aside?'

She straightened, not budging an inch. 'It's late. And, even if it weren't, you're wasting your time. You're the last person my father would want to do business with.'

His jaw shifted sideways as he leaned forward, his black eyes coming closer.

'Then obviously you have no idea *what* your father is capable of.'

His warm breath brushed her face, testosterone laced with coffee overlaid with something far more potent—

Was it ruthlessness?

Or cruelty? And for the first time her fear became tangible. Now it wasn't only the sight of him or the sound of his hard words in a smooth accent that she had to deal with; now she had the very essence of him assailing her lungs, assaulting her senses, testing her sanity.

And it was too much.

In spite of the balmy autumn night she could feel the heated moisture break out on her forehead; she could feel every muscle tightening in preparation for fight or flight.

What had brought this man here tonight? Why would he possibly think he would be offered entrée into their house— after doing his utmost to bring her family and two hundred years of history crumbling down with them?

Right now, it didn't matter. Because there was one thing sh[e] registered instinctively—that, whatever this man was doing her[e] no good could come of it. And he'd made her family suffe[r] enough as it was.

The answer was as patently simple as it was critical. Diabl[o] Barrentes wouldn't cross this threshold, not while she rode shotgu[n.]

'Briar? Who is it, dear?'

Surprised her mother was still awake, she still only let he[r] head tilt slightly in the direction of her voice. There was n[o] way she was taking her eyes off the dark nemesis before her[.] 'It's no one important. I've taken care of it.' And with a rus[h] of satisfaction she reached for the handle and attempted to ram the door home.

She didn't even come close. Like a lightning bolt, his hand shot out, palm flat and long fingers outstretched, arresting the path of the heavy door dead. Then, with just one cast-iron shove, he pushed it right back and clean out of her grasp.

'What do you think you're doing?' she cried out in both fury and shock as the door swung wildly past her, leaving him standing exposed in the open doorway like some angry black spider determined that its meal was not going to escape.

'Briar!' her mother cried, her voice tense and sharp as a rapier. 'Let Mr Barrentes in.'

She turned to face her mother fully this time. 'You can't be serious. Not after—'

'I *am* serious,' the older woman said in barely more than a whisper, one arm held tight around her chest, the fingers of her other hand nervously clutching at her throat. 'Your father's been expecting him. Come in, Mr Barrentes. Cameron's waiting for you in the library. I apologise for my daughter's lack of decorum.'

Briar reeled as if she'd been slapped in the face. But her mother had a point. So much for her Davenport breeding; it had gone out the door the moment she'd opened it, no match at all for dealing with a man like Diablo.

'It's quite all right,' he said, striding past Briar's stunned form with barely an acknowledgement. 'I find there's nothing I enjoy more these days than a woman with spirit.'

Her mother closed her eyes and seemed to sway on her feet for a moment. 'Quite,' she said, after recovering her composure, not quite able or willing to meet her daughter's concerned gaze. 'Well, if you come this way, Mr Barrentes…'

'What's going on?'

Carolyn Davenport turned to her daughter, or rather *almost* to her, focusing on a point somewhere over her shoulder.

'Perhaps you could close the door, dear; there's a real chill in the air tonight. Then maybe you could get the men some coffee and brandy? I'm sure they have plenty to discuss.'

Her mother had to be kidding. If there was a chill in the air it had more to do with the black cloud she'd just admitted into the house rather than the ambient temperature. And be damned if she'd serve what little was left of the good brandy to the likes of Diablo Barrentes, the man who'd almost single-handedly cost one of the oldest and most respected Sydney families its fortune.

'I'll get my father anything he needs,' she conceded, swinging the door closed, realising she was abandoning any hint of good breeding and yet unable to stop herself. 'But I'm sorry, Mother, Diablo can fend for himself.'

Half an hour later she was still simmering over the presence of their unwanted guest when her mother found her sitting alone in the kitchen.

'Has he gone?' she asked.

Her mother shook her head and Briar felt her blood pressure spike before forcing her attention back to the screen. Not that she could concentrate when her head was full of one take-no-prisoners Spaniard. Damn the man! What could he possibly want of her father now? There was nothing left for him to take. Even the family home—the last remaining asset—was now mortgaged to the hilt.

'What are you doing, sweetheart?' her mother asked as she came around behind her, placing a hand on her shoulder and stroking with gentle pressure. Briar smiled as she leaned her head into the caress, feeling some of her tension dissipate under her mother's touch.

'It's that schedule I've been working on, listing the furniture and artworks you and Dad decided you could bear to part with. I've spoken to the auctioneer and, rather than sending everything off in one big lot, it looks like if we send the right pieces to auction every two or three months, we'll still have enough to meet our commitments.'

'Oh? Is that right?' Her mother's hand stopped moving and she shifted to the stool alongside, the tight frown that marred her brow as she contemplated the detail of the spreadsheet's contents adding at least ten years to her age.

And suddenly Briar regretted her earlier behaviour at the front door. Carolyn Davenport had been barely more than a shell of her former self lately, her skin pale and drawn, her emotions brittle. The stress of their money troubles was taking its toll on all of them, but on none more so than on her mother, who was still feeling the loss of her eldest child two years before. Almost too reluctant to venture downtown any more, she'd been constantly humiliated by the newspaper articles documenting the family's downfall and the endless pitying looks from one-time society friends. And, despite the provocation of the most arrogant male in the world, Briar hadn't helped the situation by behaving more like a teenager in a snit than the twenty-four-year-old woman she was.

With a few quick clicks of her finger, she saved the spreadsheet and closed down the computer. Being reminded of the family heirlooms that would soon no longer be theirs was no doubt the last thing her mother needed right now. 'Don't worry; I'm sure it's not as bad as it looks. We'll work our way through this, I know we will. And if that job I was promised at the gallery comes through, things will be even better.'

Her mother placed her hand over hers and patted it lightly. 'You're so good to do all of this. And with any luck we might not have to sell everything after all. Your father's hoping there might just be another way out of this mess.'

Briar swivelled around to face her mother, her hands held palms up. 'But what else is there? We've done the rounds of the banks and the financiers; we've tried everything going. I thought we'd run out of options.'

'All except one,' she said, her eyes taking on a sudden spark. 'Just today it seems we've been offered something of a lifeline. The loans paid off and a settlement—a large one, enough for us to get the staff back and live like we used to, without having to sell everything and scrimp and save. It'll be just like before— like nothing ever happened. Except...' Her mother's fast and furious speech ran down as she turned her head in the direction of the library, a look of bleakness extinguishing the spark, turning her eyes grey and cold, frosty needles ascended Briar's spine.

'Oh, no! You can't mean Diablo? Please tell me this has nothing to do with why *that* man is here tonight.'

Her mother didn't answer and despair pumped unchallenged through her system. She launched herself off her stool and put her hands up in protest. 'But this is all his fault! He's almost single-handedly brought about the downfall of the Davenport family. Why should he then turn around and offer help? It makes no sense. There's nothing left for him to take.'

Her mother stood and came closer, tucking one renegade tendril of hair behind her daughter's ear before running her hands down her arms, squeezing them at her elbows. 'Right now we're hardly in a position to be choosy.'

'But he's so awful! The way he swaggers around Sydney like he owns the place.'

Her mother raised her eyebrows on a breath. 'Well, these days that's probably somewhere close to the truth.' She smiled weakly. 'But just think, he can't be all bad. He must have some redeeming features, don't you think?'

Briar snorted. 'They're well and truly hidden if he has.'

'And he is a very good-looking man.'

'I guess, if you go for the bandit look.' She frowned, the direction her mother's arguments were taking suddenly niggling at her. 'Anyway, we're talking about Diablo Barrentes. The same Diablo Barrentes who has set out to bring down the Sydney establishment, and the Davenport family first and foremost. What's it matter what he loo—'

'Briar—' her father's gruff tones interrupted them from behind '—I'm glad you're still up. Can you spare me a minute or two?'

She breathed a sigh of relief. Her father's appearance meant Diablo must have gone at last, and good riddance to him. She was sick of feeling on tenterhooks in her own home. And at least now she might find out what was going on. If her father was planning on accepting help from Diablo, she'd have a few things to say about it first.

'You go with your father,' her mother urged, her smile too thin, too unconvincing, as she gestured towards the door. 'We've finished anyway.'

She caught the loaded look that passed between her parents. Something was going on. Why didn't her parents look happier if there was a lifeline in the offing?

Or were Barrentes's terms too costly?

A sick feeling snaked in her gut. Nothing would surprise her. Diablo would be sure to want to stick the boot in now that he had her father down.

Damn the man. She'd do everything possible to ensure they could avoid his greedy clutches.

'Actually,' her mother piped up, catching her daughter's hand in a sudden change of heart, 'maybe I should come along with you.'

'No!' insisted Cameron, insinuating himself between the two women and breaking their grasp. 'You stay here,' he directed at his wife. 'This won't take long. And then I could probably use another coffee.'

'So are you ever going to tell me what's going on?' Briar asked her father a few moments later, wishing he would say something—*anything*—as he led her through the house. His silence was unsettling. 'What did Diablo want?'

Just outside the library he paused and turned to her, taking both her hands in his, the look on his face almost one of defeat, and this close up she was shocked to see how dark and heavy those circles under his eyes really were. It might be late but it was clear the stress of their circumstances was eating away at him, too. From inside the library the old grandfather clock ticked away the seconds ominously.

'Briar,' he said on a sigh, 'before we go any further, I want you to know that I didn't want this to happen, you have to believe that.' He peered at her so intently she could feel his utter desperation, his bony hands cold and unsettlingly clammy around her own.

She swallowed. 'You didn't mean what to happen?'

'I need you help,' he continued, evading her question, 'even though I know that what I am asking of you may be too much.'

'It's okay,' she replied with a confidence she didn't feel, squeezing his hands back. She tried desperately to raise a smile but a racing heart and a mind filled with shadows and creeping foreboding wouldn't let her. 'So what is it you want me to do?'

A dark flicker of movement wrenched her attention away from her father as a prickle of awareness skittered along her skin.

Diablo! So he hadn't left after all! And now he stood leaning casually against the doorway. Although the look on his face was anything but.

Victory, his features proclaimed.

It was there in the dangerous glint in his eyes. It was there in the voracious tilt of his smile. And it was there in the menacing darkness of his attitude.

'It's really quite simple,' Diablo announced, answering for her father, his teeth flashing dangerously as he levered himself away from the door and closer to her.

'Your father merely expects you to marry me.'

CHAPTER TWO

'IF THAT'S your idea of a joke, Mr Barrentes...' Briar's voice sounded strangely calm in spite of the explosions going off behind her eyes '...I'd say you were seriously overdue for a sense of humour transplant.'

He laughed. Or rather he rumbled, that low rolling sound that vibrated uncomfortably through her.

She bristled, trying to dispel the rush of heat that came with his proximity. 'I'm afraid I don't see the joke.'

His mouth quietened, his eyes stilled. *On hers.* 'That's because it is no joke. Your father has agreed that you will marry me.'

For a moment she was speechless. But only for a moment. Then it was her turn to laugh, wiping away his wild assertions with a sweep of one hand. 'You're crazy! Dad, tell him how ludicrous he sounds. There's no way you'd ever expect me to do something so absurd as to marry someone like *him*.' She looked at her father, inviting him to agree—*imploring him to agree*—but her father said nothing, his eyes more desolate than she'd ever seen them, and the laughter died on her lips just as hope died in her heart.

'Briar,' he said in the bare bones of a whisper, reaching for her shoulder, 'you have to understand—'

A hitched moment of realisation passed and then, *'No!'* She recoiled from both his touch and from what his eyes told her. 'There's nothing to understand.'

'Please,' her father pleaded, 'before you mother hears us.' He motioned them both into the room before closing the door behind them. 'You must listen to me.'

Her mind a blur, she let herself be bustled inside the room before she turned on her father, blurting out just how she felt. 'How can I listen when what you say makes no sense?'

'And how can you say it makes no sense,' Diablo argued from the sidelines, one arrogant eyebrow cocked, 'if you don't listen?'

She snapped her head around in his direction. 'If I'd wanted your opinion, I would have asked for it.'

He didn't look nonplussed. Far from it. In fact he looked altogether too pleased with himself as he leant back against her father's desk, his hands planted wide either side of him, pulling his shirt taut across a muscled chest that looked far better than any man's had a right to. The open V of his shirt revealed olive skin that was impossibly smooth, almost glossy, and a hint of dark chest hair. She forced her eyes higher, aware that she'd been staring. Her mother was right. Diablo Barrentes was one good-looking man. Why did someone so detestable have to be blessed with such good looks and such a killer body? There was clearly no justice in this world.

He smiled then, as if amused by what her face betrayed of her thoughts. 'You are as prickly as your name suggests, my wild rose.'

'I am *not* your wild rose! Don't you understand? I don't want to marry you. And there's no way on earth you can make me.'

She turned her attention back to her father as another cog suddenly slipped into place. Suddenly her mother's 'he must have some redeeming features' discussion made sense, though not the sudden secrecy. 'What's this really about? Why did you make us come into the library? Mother knows about this arrangement, doesn't she?'

Her father looked grey. 'She knows something of the proposal, it's true.'

Briar's gut churned. '*Something of the proposal*'? What more could there possibly be? What she was hearing already set her stomach roiling. And the very concept that her future had been mapped out by her own parents—the two people she'd always assumed loved her and wanted the best for her—was too much.

'So you've discussed this then, between yourselves like some kind of domestic transaction. I can just imagine how the conversation went: *"Shall we renovate the beach house? Maybe trade up to the new Mercedes? Oh, and while we're at it, maybe we can marry Briar off to Diablo Barrentes."*'

She swivelled her head and firmly fixed Diablo in her sights. 'You've worked out between yourselves that you're going to marry me off to the person this family detests more than anyone in the world. How could you do that?'

Diablo didn't flinch at her words, his eyes merely glinting menacingly. Her father, however, was getting more agitated.

'Briar, calm down, we have no choice!'

'There's always a choice! Like I have a choice. Because there's no way I'm marrying Diablo Barrentes. I wouldn't marry him if he was the last man on earth.' She swung around in Diablo's direction and looked square into his dark fathomless eyes. 'I'd rather die!'

This time the merest tic in his cheek was the only indication that her words had met their mark. 'It's drama you studied at university, then,' he delivered in a tone that told her how unimpressed he was with the proceedings. 'I was obviously under a misapprehension.'

'I studied fine arts,' she hissed. 'Not that it's any business of yours.'

He raised his eyebrows. 'You surprise me, given you have such a flair for the dramatic.'

'And you have such a flair for the insane! How could you possibly imagine I would marry you? What were you thinking? That you could marry your way into Sydney society? It won't work. People aren't going to forget how you rode roughshod over everyone in your path to get to where you are today.'

He surveyed her through half-hooded eyes that failed to hide those dark simmering depths. 'You resent me for building my own fortune, instead of having it bestowed on me through some accident of birth like you and your kind?'

'I resent you because you've built your fortune by pulling others down, my father included.'

'Is that so? And yet now I'm offering your father a chance to get re-established. He can see the sense in the offer. And yet still you resent me.'

'I will *always* resent you.'

She turned in frustration to her father. 'Please, tell me this is all a joke. You can't really expect me to marry this arrogant Spanish import. This is twenty-first century Sydney, after all. We don't do arranged marriages!'

Her father shook his head sadly. 'Briar...' His voice choked off as he sank down into an armchair, dropping his head into his hands. 'Oh God, I've been such a fool.'

She rushed to him and knelt at his side, latching both hands on to his forearm, willing him some of her strength and hope. 'Dad, listen to me. We don't need Diablo's money. I've got it all worked out. We can survive just like we planned—with my job and by auctioning the good furniture periodically. We don't need to go crawling to people like him. We don't need his money.'

'It's not that easy,' her father murmured, shaking his head from side to side.

'It *is* that easy,' she assured him. 'We don't have to make this deal. I haven't had a chance to tell you yet—because we can survive without it. So what that we won't have servants?—We can cope. We've been coping. And I'll have a job soon.'

'We're not coping! Look at the state of the house—it's killing your mother that she can't keep up with everything.'

'Who cares if the floors don't get cleaned every day? Things will get better, you'll see.'

Her father grabbed her by the shoulders, his desperate fingers clawing into her flesh so hard it hurt. With his hurt, she knew. 'No, it's not that easy,' he reiterated. 'You have to listen. We have no money left. No credit. Nothing.'

'We do,' she argued, wanting to stop his pain. 'Or we will, and enough to keep us going and to get us through these times. We don't need anyone else's money, let alone his. Let me go and get the schedule I've been working on. I'll prove it to you. I've worked it all out.'

'Briar,' was all he said as he dropped his grip to her hands, holding on to them for all he was worth, not letting her rise. 'Thank you. You're such a good child. I'm so proud of you.'

She looked into her father's eyes and saw his approval beaming out at her. She relished the moment as he pulled her close, wrapping her securely in his arms, and for a moment they were the only two people in the room. Nobody else counted. Nobody else mattered. Her father thought he had been carrying the entire burden of their debt on his shoulders. Now he knew that Briar had also been searching for solutions. And everything would look different when he'd seen her calculations. She'd soon show him they didn't need to resort to people like Diablo for the funds to ensure their future.

'So when are you going to tell her?' jarred a voice from outside her perfect understanding. And she stilled within the circle of her father's arms as dread turned her blood to ice.

'Tell me what?' she asked huskily, drawing back to search her father's face. What the hell else could there be?

He looked down at her with his empty eyes and it was impossible not to feel his despair drape around her, damp and pungent. 'There's nothing left.'

'What do you mean?' she asked, willing life into his eyes, searching for the merest flicker of hope. '"Nothing left"?'

'It's all gone. All of it.'

'But we've still got the house and the furniture! I told you…'

But, even as she was speaking, his head was shaking from side to side.

'Gone,' her father said. 'All that was left is gone. It's Diablo's now. Everything. The house, the furniture. Everything.'

Fury took charge of her senses. She rose up and wheeled around. 'You bastard!' She moved closer. Never before had she had an urge to tear someone limb from limb but tonight was becoming a night for firsts. Her first arranged marriage. Her first fiancé. Why not her first homicide? She lifted one hand, resisting the desire to lash out at his smug face, instead curling it into a fist between them.

'You scheming bastard. Not content to obliterate four generations of work, you couldn't let up until you had taken every last thing, even our family home, and consigned us to the gutter. What a hero. Do you feel proud of yourself now?'

In the space of a blink he'd ensnared her wrist, the heat from his grip like a brand on her arm.

'I'm offering a way to keep you all out of that gutter. I've told your father—he can keep the house and everything in it along with a sizeable lump of cash every year. All you have to do is be that good daughter your father seems to think you are. All you have to do is marry me and all your family's unfortunate financial problems will be a thing of the past.'

The grip around her wrist tightened, forcing her towards him, closer to his dark eyes and his tight body and his masculine heat. If his gaze at the door had been sizzling hot, his hold and his closeness was like an incendiary device set to slow burn. Already her skin sizzled into life; how long would it take to get to flash-point?

'Put like that, it seems you leave me no choice,' she said through gritted teeth, watching his eyes flare with an anticipated victory.

'I'm glad you're willing to see reason at last,' he said, loosening his grip.

'Oh, yes, I see reason. I'll take the gutter over you any day!'

She took advantage of his shock by wrenching her arm free, massaging the burning skin as she wheeled away.

'You don't know what you're letting yourself in for!' Diablo countered. 'You have no idea what it's like to live in poverty, always desperate to find your next meal, never able to make ends meet, and with your pampered upbringing you won't survive ten minutes out in the real world.'

She spun on her heel, lifted her chin determinedly. 'Oh, we'll survive.'

He scoffed. 'What—you see yourself as the noble poor? Allow me to let you in on a secret—there are no noble poor. There are only the poor, the hungry and the desperate. There's no place for nobility in that line-up. The gutter is no fairy tale romantic notion.'

She regarded him levelly. 'What a coincidence,' she mustered. 'Neither, it seems, is marrying you.' She turned to where her father still sat, looking like an empty shell of a man, a fallen ruler, vanquished and heartsick for what he'd lost, and pain for what he was feeling now encompassed her like a tide rolling in.

'I'm sorry, Dad. I can't do it. I just can't marry him.'

Her father nodded his head and she knew that it was not in agreement but in resignation. He seemed to shrink before her eyes. 'I understand,' he croaked. 'I should never have had to ask you. It's all my fault—my fault. Now I just have to find a way of telling your mother that we no longer have a home.'

Briar's heart plummeted.

'Oh, God, you mean she doesn't know? I thought she must have been in on this crazy idea.'

'She doesn't know we've lost Blaxlea. I didn't want to worry her unnecessarily. But now…'

'Oh, Dad, no…'

The grandfather clock clicked loudly in the ensuing silence as the mechanism for the chimes kicked in, the prelude for ringing out the midnight hour.

Diablo strode between them. 'Can you do that to your mother, then? Deny her the chance to see out her days in this house rather than some doss-house? What kind of a daughter are you really?'

She said nothing, just let her eyes tell him how much she hated him while inside her heart ached for her mother. Because Diablo was right—how could she do that to her mother after what she'd been through? After losing Nat, then the business and along with it their fortune, to lose the family home would kill her.

'I can see you need more time to think about it,' Diablo decided. 'So I'm prepared to give you one more chance. You have until the clock strikes twelve to decide once and for all. Marry me and your family live in comfort for the rest of their days. Turn me down and you'll be out of this house by the end of the week.'

'You can't do that!'

'Watch me,' he said. 'It's not as if you have anything left to pack.'

'Even you couldn't be so cold-hearted!'

'It's not up to me any more,' he said as the clock finished its chimes and made the first of twelve strikes. 'It's up to you what happens next. Luxury or poverty, it's your call. Will you abandon your parents in their hour of need or will you restore your parents to the life they desire?'

The clock struck again. 'That's two,' he said. 'I hope you're thinking.'

Oh, she was thinking all right. Panicked thoughts with no beginning and no end and no hope. And, between them all, the clock struck again.

Would it kill her to marry him? Maybe not, but there was no doubt it would definitely kill her mother to leave Blaxlea, her childhood home and the seat of her mother's family for generations.

And would she ever forgive Briar for rejecting the financial lifeline that Diablo was now offering?

The clock struck again and she looked up in panic. Had she missed one? How much time was left? There was too much to consider.

Why, oh, why, did it all have to come down to her? *Oh Nat,* she pleaded, *what should I do?* But she knew without question that if her big brother had survived the crash that had cut short his life, he wouldn't hesitate to help. He'd do whatever it took to help his parents out, even if it meant sacrificing his own career and his own future into the deal. So why did the thought of sacrificing her own chances seem so abhorrent? After all, all she had to do was to marry Diablo.

Marriage…

The clock sounded again, straining her nerves to breaking-point. It was almost time.

Marriage sounded so final. But then hadn't she always planned on getting married one day? Indeed, she'd been groomed from the day she was born for being a society wife with a rich husband… Would it really matter if it was to Diablo? And it didn't have to be for ever. He'd get sick of her before too long—she'd make sure of it—and then he'd have to agree to divorce her. How long would it take—one year? Two? She'd make sure there were no children to suffer in the fallout. And then she'd have her life back. It wouldn't kill her. Marrying Diablo didn't have to be a life sentence.

All too soon it was just an echo that rolled around the room. The clock had rung out for the last time. The witching hour was here—the time when bad things crawled out of the night and ruled supreme. Diablo, the Spanish devil, was nothing if not faithful to the old legends.

She looked across at her father, who sat there looking like the beaten man he was. He looked up at her as if he'd realised too that this was it, his eyes bearing a rare spark of defiance. 'Don't do it,' he urged in a gruff entreaty as he rose to his feet, some measure of his fighting spirit renewed. 'This is my fault—all of it. You shouldn't have to pay for my mistakes. We'll make it through somehow.'

She smiled and mouthed a silent thank you.

'Well?' demanded the Spanish devil, drawing closer, obviously impatient to seal the deal. 'What have you decided?'

'That I hate you,' she snapped. 'With all my heart and soul.'

He lifted a hand to her face quickly and she recoiled, but his touch, when it came, was surprisingly gentle as he ran the backs of his fingers along the line of her jaw. She shuddered at the sizzle of flesh against flesh as his eyes bored into hers, rendering her breathless, unable to move. 'Hate is such a useless waste of passion.' He sighed and turned away and she dragged in air hungrily.

'But so be it. Under the circumstances,' he stated coldly, 'I want you all packed and out of here by the end of the week.'

'No!'

He spun around. 'What do you mean, "no"? My terms were clear.'

'It means we won't be leaving.'

'Briar,' her father implored, 'don't do it. You can't—'

Diablo held up one hand that silenced her father in a heartbeat as he scrutinised her face, the barest hint of a smile returning as the dark vacuum of his bottomless eyes sucked in hers. 'Tell me,' he insisted.

She took a deep breath and prayed for strength. Because she needed strength if she was going to do this. And she had no choice *but* to do this.

For my mother, she told herself, *for my family*.

'I'll do it,' she whispered, feeling like a swimmer out of her depth, going down for the third and final time.

'I'll marry you.'

CHAPTER THREE

'WHAT's taking you so long?' asked Carolyn Davenport, bustling with excitement as she swept into Briar's room, holding her turquoise gown's ample skirts up high and trailing a silky layered train in her wake. 'It's just fabulous downstairs,' she announced. 'Everyone's here. Even with the short notice, I think the whole of Sydney society has turned out.'

Only out of morbid curiosity, thought Briar cynically as she applied the finishing touches to her make-up. No matter what story Diablo's spin doctors had concocted to release to the press, there wasn't a chance anyone believed theirs was a love match.

Anyone, that was, apart from her mother.

Carolyn Davenport had taken the news of the impending nuptials like the true society doyenne she was, swinging into mother-of-the-bride mode as if she was born to it. Any hint that she'd known about a link between her daughter's rushed marriage and the fact that now suddenly they had servants again, with the funds to pay for them and much more besides, like her brand new Lisa Ho gown, for example, seemed to have been conveniently deleted from her memory. Her mother seemed all too ready to believe in the whole sorry fairy tale.

'Fairy tale romance', *my eye,* Briar thought, reflecting on the latest headline as she snapped the blusher compact closed. But

even the business pages hadn't been immune to the press bombardment.

'*Marriage Merger*' had been their angle—'*a blending of new money with old, the brash success of the young entrepreneur merged with the proven track record of the establishment*'.

How the papers would lap it up if she came clean with her own version of the headline—'*Blackmail Bride—sold to save her family from financial ruin*'. But that story would never come out, no matter how true.

'You could do with more colour than that,' her mother protested, as Briar dropped the blusher back into a drawer. 'You look so pale tonight—I knew we should have got your make-up done professionally. Are you feeling nervous?'

'Not really.' *Feeling sick, more like it.* Briar looked briefly back in the mirror to check—even against the white silk of her simple toga-inspired gown she looked pale—but then, what make-up was going to be a match for her mood? There was only so much you could do with powder and paint.

'Never mind,' her mother said, when it was clear her daughter was going to make no attempt to redress the issue. 'I'm sure a glass of champagne will soon put some colour in your cheeks.'

Briar's stomach clamped down in rebellion. Champagne was the last thing she needed. After all, tonight was hardly a celebration.

'Come on, then,' her mother urged. 'Diablo's waiting for you downstairs. Just wait till you see him; he looks so dashing tonight.'

'That's nice,' she responded absently, slipping her feet into heels. Who cared what he looked like? He could be the most handsome man in the world, but it would still be the devil in disguise waiting for her. And frankly, he could just keep on waiting. Just because she'd agreed to marry him didn't mean that she'd be dancing to his tune any time soon.

She'd done a lot of thinking over the last two weeks and she'd worked out her own musical score for this marriage. Diablo craved respectability and an entrée to Sydney society. He didn't care about her and he almost certainly didn't even like her. Given that the feeling was mutual, it shouldn't take much to convince him that the best way to make this marriage work was for them both to lead separate lives. At least until he tired of her and agreed to a divorce. That way life might be bearable. She could put up with a year or two of inconvenience if she knew that at the other side of it she'd be free.

'Oh, hasn't Carlos done such a wonderful job with your hair?' her mother exclaimed with delight. 'It suits that gown perfectly. Although I still don't understand why you wanted to wear that old thing. It is a special occasion, after all.'

Not *that* special. And this 'old thing' was barely twelve months old and only worn once as it was. But still, she turned and smiled at her mother's never-ending enthusiasm. Someone had to be enthusiastic about this wedding and who better than her mother? Already she looked so much better than she had just two short weeks ago when this crazy marriage plan had been unleashed, her features less drawn, her frown vanquished. It wasn't just that their financial situation had taken a turn for the better, she knew, but because her mother genuinely seemed to want this marriage to work out.

'I'm just saving my splurge for the big event,' she told her, with a passion she didn't feel, taking her mother's arm and pulling her in close. 'Come on, let's go meet these guests.'

The champagne flowed so freely it seemed the huge ballroom was awash with it. Champagne, old money and the celebrity A-List blended together in the Blaxlea ballroom, which fairly gleamed since the team of cleaners Diablo had organised to go over the place had done their bit. Huge arrangements of flowers were doubled in the enormous mirrors, their colours reflected in the crystal chandeliers, while a full wall of feature windows welcomed in the diamond lights of Sydney Harbour at night.

It was some place all right and it could have been his outright—indeed it had been, for just one night. But he was happy with his deal—they could keep the title to the house. Tonight he would gain himself something much more important than just bricks and mortar and a few hundred feet of prime Sydney Harbour frontage. Tonight he'd cement his place and his future with the society that had resisted him for so long.

Already he could sense the change in the way he was perceived, by the constant string of congratulations he'd received from people who would have crossed the street to avoid him in the past, as he stood alongside Cameron Davenport waiting for the ladies to appear. In marrying Briar there was no way they could ignore his hold on the Sydney property industry any more. Now he had the Davenport seal of approval. Now there would be no stopping him.

How fortunate that a man so unskilled in the ways of his business should have had such a suitable daughter. For there was no one he'd rather cement his future with than Briar Davenport. She would make the perfect wife. The bonus was she would also make a pleasant bed-warmer. Siring children with her would be no hardship.

There was a stir amongst the crowd before everyone hushed and his eyes drifted upwards to where the two women stood at the top of the stairs, the older woman in plumage peacock-bold, the daughter so deathly pale as to render any other mere mortal invisible.

But not Briar. Her skin might be pale but her eyes shone like dream stones, amber and intense. And the dress might be colourless but it could not disguise the exquisitely feminine form beneath. A tiny waist that only accentuated the lushness of her breasts and hips, and legs that went forever and then some.

Briar. Like the rose that grew wild, spreading branches rambling, *soon she would be clambering all over him.* Already he could feel those long limbs wrapped around him, clinging to him, supported by him. Already he could hear her crying out, begging him for release. His body stirred in anticipation as the women slowly descended the wide staircase.

Oh, no, siring children with her would be no hardship at all.

The women reached the foot of the stairs. Carolyn took her husband's arm. Diablo held out his hand for Briar and for the first time she looked at him.

Something jolted through her as their eyes connected, a prelude for the bolt of electricity that was unleashed when their hands touched. His dark eyes narrowed and regarded her strangely.

'You look beautiful,' he said. 'Like a virgin sacrifice about to be tossed to the lions.'

How appropriate, she thought, though hardly willing to buy into that particular discussion. 'And you,' she replied, 'look like the proverbial cat that got the cream.'

He drew her hand closer, pressing his mouth, warm and moist, to her skin while his eyes held hers. 'Not yet; so far I only have the unopened package. But, I must confess, I'm looking forward to opening it up and then—' his eyes narrowed and focused like dark torchlight '—and then sampling the treasure within.'

She dragged in air and turned her head away, suddenly too uncomfortable, too giddy, too *hot*. She didn't need a mirror to tell her that there was plenty of colour in her cheeks now. Diablo's words had achieved in an instant what the finest cosmetics in the world had failed to do.

Yet it wasn't just his words heating her body. Her mother hadn't been exaggerating. Tonight he looked magnificent in clothes that would have made a lesser man look ridiculous and yet on Diablo merely accentuated his masculine power. A snow-white shirt contrasted with his smooth olive skin and black fitted trousers that finished above hand-stitched leather boots. Over it all he wore a long black jacket with a Nehru collar that emphasized his long, lean length. With his hair tied back, all he needed was a gold hoop in his earlobe and he could have been a pirate out on the town celebrating his latest conquest.

And, if that wasn't enough, just breathing the same air, laced with the heady tang of his aftershave, was like getting a shot of testosterone.

And damn him but somehow that scent was like a lure, snagging on her defences, tangling with her resistance. Purposefully she stiffened her spine. She would not be attracted to such a man. It couldn't happen.

Someone—her father—made a toast and the room erupted into applause and congratulations. Briar made out not a word of it as she scanned the crowded ballroom without taking in a thing. She was too busy working out what to do next. They would have to talk—privately—and soon. Diablo had to be made to see under what terms she was prepared to marry him and that those terms in no way included him sampling *anything*!

'Darling? Briar?'

It was hearing her name that brought her back and she turned to him, ready to protest that she was hardly his darling, but something in his eyes stopped her in her tracks.

'Didn't you hear the guests? They're waiting for us to seal our betrothal with a kiss.'

And, before she could protest this latest indignity, that there was no way she would kiss him, least of all in front of two hundred people, his mouth was on hers and any protest was muffled, *melted*, by the sheer impact of his lips.

They were soft, she realised with surprise—soft but sure. He looked so powerful dressed as he was all in black, hard and unyielding, and yet his lips moved over hers with an elegance of movement and a grace that was as surprising as it was intoxicating.

Heat rolled through her in waves, a surging tide of warmth that crashed and foamed into her extremities and set her flesh to tingling and her protests all but forgotten. The room shrank around them until there was just this kiss, these sensations, this mouth, weaving magic on hers.

And then he lifted his mouth from hers and sounds and colour and people invaded her numbed senses once more. She blinked as the crowd cheered; she blinked as her state of daze sloughed away; she blinked as Diablo smiled back at her, success lining that passionate slash of mouth, as she realised what she'd done.

Dear God! She'd let Diablo Barrentes kiss her, in public. And his expression told her he was gloating about it. She lifted one hand, touched the back of it to lips that still hummed from his touch, but he stilled the movement, pulling her hand down within his.

'You don't wipe me away that easily.'

She didn't doubt it, her mouth still full of the taste of him.

'We have to talk,' she croaked as her parents were absorbed into a circle of guests and a buzz of conversation went up all around them. 'Tonight. In private.'

The spark in his eyes flared, one dark eyebrow lifted in surprise. 'I did not expect you to be so accommodating quite so readily.'

Already rattled by his kiss, she was in no mood for his easy confidence.

'We have to *talk*! We need to set down some ground rules for this arrangement.'

He took two glasses of champagne from a passing waiter's tray, handing her one. 'Oh? That sounds very important.' He took a bored sip of his wine that told her he thought it sounded anything but. 'In that case we will talk. But later.' He took her free hand, surrounding it in his warmth, and headed into the ballroom. 'First the happy couple must mingle with our guests seeing they've come especially to wish us well.'

'You mean they've come to knit at my execution. They're

nothing but ghouls, wanting to witness the ultimate degradation of one of their own.'

He stopped dead and lowered his head to hers, his body close, his voice a clipped whisper in her ear. 'You had a choice. You did not have to agree to this.'

'I had *no* choice, and you know it. You left me without any choice at all.'

'Wrong,' he hit back. 'You could have walked away from me and—' he swept his champagne-bearing hand around the room '—and all of this.'

'I couldn't—'

'No! You could have, but you *didn't*—for whatever reasons you had, you chose not to! And, having made your decision, I expect you to live with it. Now, I suggest we meet some of our guests.'

It was many hours and many more cases of champagne later that the party wound down, leaving only a few of Cameron's colleagues, who seemed all too content to settle in for brandy and cigars in the library. Carolyn had excused herself an hour ago, pleading too much excitement, and Briar sympathised.

It had seemed an endless night, moving on from one group of people to the next, filling the time with the same small talk, trying to instil the right measure of excitement into her voice. She could see the doubts, she could see the cynical way half the attendees accepted the marriage, the questions they asked, aimed to find any chink in the story, seeking out the truth they knew was there if they just dug in the right place.

She could even see the looks of envy that were fired her way from women who obviously thought Diablo was some kind of catch. Just because he hadn't been embraced by Sydney society didn't mean there wasn't a queue of women lining up to be photographed on his arm.

Diablo had carried himself through the night like a consummate professional, letting his answers trip from his tongue—*their attraction had surprised them both but now they couldn't wait to be married, and the icing on the cake was his father-in-law-to-be's sudden change in fortunes.*

And all the while he'd bluffed his way through the potential minefield of the evening, he'd never let her stray more than inches away, his arm proprietorialy looped over her shoulders or around her waist, or just reaching out to stroke her arm, or tuck a strand of hair away from her face. Briar, on the other hand, had smiled through gritted teeth at the pointed questions and gentle caresses and wished the whole evening over. After what felt like an eternity, thankfully, it nearly was.

'Now, you wanted to talk.'

They had just bid farewell to the last of the departing guests at the front door. She shook her head, revelling in being able to put some distance between them at last. At last the pretence was over. But the strain of deflecting their barbed queries coupled with Diablo's constant presence at her side had left her with such a thundering tension headache that all she wanted to do now was to go to bed. The last thing she wanted to face was an all too revealing statement of how she saw their marriage working.

'It can wait,' she conceded, rubbing her temples. 'I'm just glad this farce of an evening is over.'

But Diablo was talking to a passing waiter and she didn't think he'd heard her.

'Why do you call it that?' he said, turning back to her a moment later and proving her assumption wrong. 'Our engagement is no farce, nor will our marriage be.'

'You know it's a farce! And having to pretend that this relationship is anything other than the business transaction it is, it's just impossible.'

His eyes narrowed. 'You think this marriage is merely a business transaction?'

'Isn't it? It's hardly a love match.'

He ushered her into a small sitting room opposite the ballroom just as the waiter returned, bearing a tray with two glasses, one a tumbler of what looked like Scotch, the other a tall frosty glass, its contents sparkling. He lifted them both from the tray and held out the tall glass as the waiter exited, closing the door behind them.

'What is it?' she said, not taking it.

'Drink it. It's an old Spanish headache remedy. It will make you feel better.'

Briar eyed the glass suspiciously. There was no telling what ingredients might go into making an 'old Spanish headache remedy'. 'And you care how I feel? I don't think so.'

He shrugged, still holding the glass even as he took a sip from his own. 'You would rather keep your headache?'

She murmured her thanks as she took the glass, aware she was being churlish, wondering at his ability to rub her up the wrong way. She sniffed tentatively at the glass, took a sip and, with surprise, instantly recognised the slightly bitter taste of paracetamol. 'Old Spanish headache remedy' indeed. She lifted her eyes to meet his and found them creased at the edges, a smirk tugging at his mouth.

He was laughing at her.

'Now,' he continued, 'let's stop wasting time. Tell me about these "ground rules" you're so keen on implementing.'

'Do we have to do this now?' she protested, after finishing the contents of her glass. She wasn't up to going ten rounds with anyone right now—let alone with Diablo. 'It's late. Can't it wait?'

'No. We will be married in two weeks and for much of that time I have business overseas. If you want anything incorporated into our pre-nuptial agreement, then you best tell me now.'

His cold words broke over her like a rogue wave, catching her unawares, tumbling her into the sandy depths. 'What pre-nuptial agreement?'

'Oh, come, come.' He swept away her protest with one potent hand. 'Surely you didn't expect we would be married without one? As you say, ours is hardly a love match.'

For a moment she bristled at his ready agreement with her summation. Only then common sense prevailed. If his terms for this marriage could be in writing, so too could hers. Two could play at that game.

'Of course, you're right,' she conceded, feeling a surge of confidence. 'A pre-nuptial agreement would be for the best. Then we both know where we stand.'

He downed the rest of his drink in one mouthful and she watched as he swirled the smooth liquor around his mouth and kick back his jaw as he sent it southwards. And through it all his eyes smouldered, never shifting from her, as if weighing her up, evaluating her.

'*Sí*, exactly. So tell me, Briar, where do you stand? What terms would you like included in the arrangement that outlines our future life together?'

'You mean our marriage together,' she corrected.

He smiled in a way that made her shiver. 'I said what I meant. Now it's your turn.'

She swung around and laced her fingers together, taking a couple of breaths before she was ready to face that bottomless dark gaze once more. She could feel her colour rising again and gave thanks for the low lighting. What she had to say was difficult enough without one hundred watts to illuminate it. 'It's really quite simple,' she began, turning. 'As you agreed, this marriage is hardly a love match. And, in that case, I think it's sensible that we understand what we bring to the marriage—in your case, it's money. In mine, it's my family connections.'

She hesitated. Diablo's body language as he sprawled into one of the wing-chairs and looked up at her was not giving anything away.

'You think all you have to offer is your family connections?'

'Isn't that the reason you came up with this plan?'

He said nothing. Just surveyed her some more. In apparently excruciating detail. Her skin bristled with irritation under his deep-seated gaze, her senses fusing.

'Go on,' he urged at last, without bothering to answer her question.

'So I've come up with a plan as to how we're going to work this out. Clearly, we have no choice now but to go ahead with this marriage but, equally clearly, it's obvious that neither of us is completely happy about the arrangement.'

'Says who?'

'Says both of us! We're both doing this out of necessity, nothing more. And, like the performance I put on tonight, I want you to know that I'm prepared to put on a public face after we're married that says we're man and wife.'

'How accommodating of you.'

'Well, I understand how important this is to you—and to me and my family. I'll do my best to make it work, to give a convincing performance as your wife.'

'And in private?'

'I beg your pardon?'

'You talked about how things would be in public. I'm wondering what you have in mind for our private life, when nobody else is watching.'

The heat continued to build under her skin. Of course, he wasn't about to make this easy for her. She stiffened her back, kicking up her chin resolutely. 'Then we live our lives separately, just as we have until entering this sham of a marriage. In public I agree to play your wife, even your adoring wife on the occasions that demand it. Out of the public eye we will lead separate lives. If you want this marriage of convenience to satisfy your need for connections, then so you shall have it, but you can't expect anything more.'

His only response was a blink of his eyes, slow and loaded. Then he leaned forward.

'And just how separate a life do you expect to lead while you occupy my bed?'

She snorted, outraged at the idea. 'That's just it. I won't be. Given your track record, I'm sure you'll have no trouble finding yourself someone who is more willing in that department. All that I ask is that you be discreet about it.'

He brushed aside her slur with a shake of his head. 'You haven't thought this through.'

'Of course I have…'

'No. Clearly you have missed something. For how are you to bear my children if you won't at least share my bed? Or are you merely suggesting a much *kinkier* way of getting pregnant?'

The heat under her skin flared into a sizzle, spreading its warming tentacles out to her furthest regions. He wanted her pregnant? He wanted her to *bear his children*? *But that would mean making love with him!*

Making love with Diablo. What would that be like? All olive skin and lean muscled limbs, control and power and heat. She shivered.

'In your dreams!'

Because there must be no children to complicate this marriage, no fallout for when they divorced, as she'd already decided they would.

His smile started and ended at his lips, his eyes refusing to get involved. 'So you know about my dreams? How convenient. Because soon I won't just have you in my dreams. Soon I will have you underneath me, in my bed—or out of it, as you clearly seem to be advocating.'

She battled with shredded senses to regain some kind of foothold in this argument. But she was slipping, losing grip. She was supposed to be stating her terms. When had this become a discussion about where the act of sex itself would take place?

'Why do you try to twist everything I say? I'm trying to be reasonable here.'

'And you think it's not reasonable for a wife to bear her husband his child?'

'In normal circumstances, certainly. But this marriage is in no way normal. You know as well as I do that this arrangement is no more than a contrivance, to pay off my father's debts and to make you look better in the world.'

He paused, his eyes narrowing. 'If you say so. But think how much better I will look with a wife *and* a clutch of children. They will be half Davenports after all, socially acceptable, born into the same society that tried to keep me out for so long. Because I'm not operating under any misapprehensions—tonight I was accepted because you were on my arm. But people don't change their colours so quickly. If anything were to happen between you and me, if our marriage was to end acrimoniously without children, I have no doubt the door to Sydney high society would soon be slammed in my face once again. And I have no intention of that happening. Children are what I want and children are what you will give me.'

'So that's why you want me—as some kind of brood mare, to bear your *devil's spawn*.'

The corners of his mouth curved up. 'Are you so disappointed it's not for your sweet nature?'

She fumed with irritation. 'You can't make me sleep with you.'

He was out of his chair and before her in an instant, his stance dangerous, confronting. He reached out to her and his attitude suddenly softened. He touched fingertips to her cheek, trailing down below her chin and raising it closer. His other hand slipped around her neck.

'No,' he whispered, so close to her face she was sure he must hear the slam of her blood in her veins. 'But maybe I can convince you.'

She could hardly breathe, let alone respond, as his fingers stirred into a slow caress at her neck that left her dizzy and swaying on her heels, her headache all but forgotten under his searing touch on her bare skin. She gasped in air, his face so close that the taste of him filled her senses, and memories of those lips and a stolen kiss resurfaced into a solid, shocking need for a replay.

'You're trembling,' he said.

'I… I'm cold,' she lied.

He drew her closer, pressing his lips first to one cheek and then the other before drawing back.

'I think,' he whispered, 'it could be fun warming you up, convincing you that making love would not be such a bad thing between us.'

She pressed her eyes shut, but behind closed lids she could still see him, larger than life, supremely confident, could still feel the sensual dance of his fingers against the bare flesh of her back.

'And if you're not enough for me?' she gasped breathlessly, looking up in challenge, desperate for any kind of defence against this slow, sensual onslaught. He answered by gathering her full length against him and shock rendered her speechless. Through their clothes, she could feel his power pulsing, straining, waiting to be unleashed.

Unleashed inside her!

It wasn't just shock that kept her from protesting. It was fascination she felt, a desire to explore more of these new sensations, a yearning for something forbidden, something carnal that this man promised, that held her mute.

'Oh,' he murmured, tugging on one diamond stud in her ear with his teeth, 'I will be *more* than enough.'

And then he let her go so swiftly she almost collapsed to the ground. She spun away, panting and dizzy, not doubting him, the throb of her pulse echoing in newly awakened flesh, already aching and ready and lush.

'So,' he said so calmly that it was as if the last few minutes had never happened. 'Now that we've settled that, if you have no further suggestions for inclusions into our pre-nuptial agreement…?' He hesitated a moment or two. 'No? Then I'll see you at the wedding.'

She was still catching her breath, her heart still thudding, as he turned and swept from the room, his long coat swinging in his wake like a cape. Her skin still tingled from his touch, her senses still humming.

So much for her resolve to keep separate lives. How long would it take him to 'convince' her that her place was in his bed? She clutched her arms about her as she remembered the feel of his lean body pressed against hers and the way her own body had responded. Probably no more than five minutes based on what had just transpired.

Damn the man! But it didn't have to be the end. So it wasn't going to be as easy as she'd hoped—she'd just have to change her plans accordingly.

He might think he'd won that round, but there was still one hell of a battle to come.

It wasn't over yet!

CHAPTER FOUR

'I'M SO sorry, Briar, this is all my fault.'

Briar squeezed her father's hand as they waited for the organ music to come to an end. How strange it was that she should be the one calming him down right now.

'Don't worry, Dad,' she assured him with a confidence dredged up from somewhere. 'You had no choice.'

'But Briar—' he began.

'*None* of us had any choice,' she insisted. 'He never gave us a chance. But at least now we've managed to save Blaxlea from his clutches.'

Her father squirmed in his dark suit. 'Briar—'

But her father's words were cut off with the strains of the wedding march ringing out, signalling that it was time to walk down that aisle and meet her fate, signalling that it was time to meet her soon-to-be husband. A quiver of sensation zipped through her, leaving her blissfully numb in its wake, so that when her father tugged her forward into the church she went without resistance.

'I now pronounce you man and wife.'

It had to be a dream—a bad dream. Any second now she'd wake up in her own bed with the morning sun streaming through the curtains and this nightmare would fade with the darkness and she'd laugh at how ridiculous it had all been…

'You may kiss the bride.'

Oh, God. A brain spinning with the effects of weeks of barely sleeping suddenly clicked into gear and registered the truth.

There would be no waking up to the light. There would be no laughter. Instead her nightmare stared down at her, his dark eyes chasing away the morning, chasing away all hope. They regarded her now, the heated possession contained within terrifying as he drew closer, collecting her into his arms.

Her eyes looked too big for her face, her skin so pale and her limbs so fragile it was a wonder she didn't snap. Instead she came softly into his arms in a rustle of creamy silk, unprotesting rather than willing, and he swallowed back a sudden and totally unfamiliar urge to comfort her. But he didn't have to comfort her. She was his now. She would accept her fate eventually.

And then his mouth slanted over her cool lips and heat arced between them in a rush.

He felt the jolt that moved through her; angling her mouth into a better fit, he felt the heat suffuse her flesh, melting her to him, and suddenly his kiss took on a life of its own and anticipation of contact more carnal hummed through his senses. If she responded this readily to just a kiss, then how much more might he heat up her temperature tonight, when they were alone?

He drew back, watched the tawny colours in her eyes eddy and swirl before coolness once again iced their depths and turned them defiant and glinting like topaz. She couldn't disguise her cheeks so readily, though, the bright slashes of colour evidence that even if her spirit wanted to fight, her flesh was more than willing. It would be a pleasure seeing her skin flush all over. And then it would be more than a pleasure bringing her spirit into line.

Organ music soared through the lofty chapel as he laced her hand through his arm as they prepared to walk back down the aisle together as man and wife, the battery of bridesmaids and groomsmen her mother had organised from the ranks of cousins hanging behind. With Briar's two best friends now living overseas and unable to make the wedding, Carolyn had only been too pleased to take matters into her own hands and organise everything.

Her mother stopped them before they'd gone two paces, hugging her daughter tightly and greeting her new son with a kiss as tears of joy streamed down her face.

'If only Nat were here to see you now,' her mother cried, and Briar bit down on her bottom lip. At least he'd been saved from witnessing this humiliation. Her father added his quiet congratulations as slowly they continued down the length of the aisle, having their progress constantly interrupted by the babble of family members, friends and colleagues, all of them from the bride's side of the church.

The press had occupied Diablo's side; only now they'd vacated their seats to form a camera-wielding posse in front of them, leaving a sprinkling of actual guests on the groom's side of the church. Did this scattering of individuals constitute all of Diablo's family and friends? She'd heard that he'd lost both his parents, but what kind of man operated so alone in the world that he had so few other contacts? And while he was frequently featured in the social pages, he'd never been seen with the same woman twice. What kind of lone-wolf had she married?

She slid a glance up at him and his eyes and jaw gave her the answer in an instant. Hard. Uncompromising. *Difficult.*

No wonder he had no friends.

Then they were outside in the bright sunny afternoon and enduring what felt like a never-ending round of poses and photographs.

'Smile,' the photographers called, reminding her once more

to paste one on. Because it was expected of her. Because it was supposed to be the happiest day of her life.

But how did you smile when you'd just been bound legally to a man you hated, when you'd been forced into a marriage because you had no other choice, for without it your family would be reduced to nothing?

How did you smile when it was the last thing in the world you felt like doing?

The official photographer requested one more pose before they headed for the reception. He arranged them in yet another clinch, this time with Diablo behind, his arms circling her waist, and she stood stock-still, trying to ignore his warm breath in her hair and the tingling of her scalp. He nuzzled his face against her hair and breathed deeply.

'Mmm,' he whispered, the sound vibrating right down to her toes, 'you look and smell delicious enough to eat.'

Breath snagged in her throat as a wave of heat roiled through her. Those lips had taken her unaware during the wedding—it wasn't hard to imagine them pushing a trail southwards, kissing, suckling, devouring. She shivered. She didn't care what he thought and she most certainly didn't want to hear it or anything that reminded her of what lay ahead. She swivelled her head away from the photographers and hissed, 'Rest assured, it's not for your benefit.'

'And does that matter?' he asked, lifting one of her hands in his own and pressing his mouth to the back of it as camera flashes went off wildly all around them, desperate to catch the apparently gallant gesture. 'When it is indeed me who will benefit. Do you realise how much I am looking forward to this night, to peeling this garment away and seeing how beautiful you are underneath, how beautiful you are everywhere?'

Remnant heat from his last assault sparked inside her, flames licking sensitive flesh to life. She squeezed down on her muscles, hoping to clamp down on the effect of his words. 'How unfortunate,' she bit back unsteadily, 'that the feeling isn't mutual.'

'When the time is right,' he growled, with just a hint of aggravation, 'all of what we feel will be mutual. I am a generous lover, my wife; you will not be disappointed.'

She gasped and tried to push herself away but suddenly the air lacked oxygen, burnt up in the blast furnace atmosphere his words generated and in the stirring press of solid flesh behind her. Instead of letting her go, his grip around her waist tightened, keeping her impossibly close to him and his burgeoning hardness. Right now there was fabric between those places they touched, fabric that still seemed tissue thin, but later—later there would be nothing between their skin but air—and, later still, not even that.

The photographer signalled an end to the formal shots. 'You can let me go now,' she protested. 'We're all done.'

'No,' he disagreed, while still easing his grip around her waist enough so she could spin away in a flurry of silk and exasperation. 'We're not done—not by a long shot.'

'We're leaving in ten minutes. I want you to be ready.'

Briar jumped. If the low voice whispering in her left ear hadn't been enough reason to scatter her thoughts and send her pulse jumping, her new husband's seemingly casual gesture of running his fingers up her right arm certainly had been. She excused herself from the group of guests she was talking with and followed the path Diablo had taken from the enormous marquee that had been set up in the grounds.

'Diablo,' she said, hitching up her skirts and skipping after him as he entered the house, 'where are we going? There's a suite been prepared here. I assumed...'

He spun around and smiled suddenly, disarming her as he stopped in front of the majestic staircase. 'Is it not traditional in this country for a groom to take his new bride away for a honeymoon?'

'You know it is. But ours is hardly a traditional marriage. Our honeymoon is likely to be over before it's begun. Frankly I can't see the point.'

His smile widened. 'Oh, you will. This night is too special not to make the most of it, don't you agree?'

She didn't, as it happened. ' "*Special*" isn't exactly the word I'd use.'

'Oh, and how would you describe it, then?'

A wedding night with Diablo? She shivered as a frosty wave of trepidation washed through her. How would anyone sane not feel fear at the thought of that lean, powerful body being unleashed on her own? Ruthless in the boardroom, ruthless in his dealings with her, why would he be anything but in the bedroom? But there was no way she'd admit she was afraid. She stiffened her spine and looked him squarely in the eye. 'As a night to be endured.'

The movement in his jaw betrayed the grinding teeth below. 'You do not enjoy the sexual act? I'm surprised…' he raked his eyes over her length '…when you look purpose-built for it.'

Camera finish make-up would help to disguise her flaming cheeks, but she knew, there was nothing to disguise her thundering heartbeat. He had to be able to hear it. Just as he must have noticed the swelling of her bustline, the peaking of her nipples.

Would he feel cheated when he discovered just how inexperienced she was? Would he find it amusing and use it as yet another tool in his arsenal of humiliation?

She turned her eyes away, gathering up her skirts. 'If you've made up your mind then, I might as well go and get changed.' She'd only reached the second step when he placed a hand to her forearm, tugging her gently back.

'You don't need to change,' he said. 'I've had a bag packed for you. I want you to accompany me just the way you are.'

'But why?' she asked, shrugging her gown's skirts in her hands for emphasis. 'Why would you want me to wear my wedding gown? I'll feel ridiculous travelling in this.' She ascended another couple of steps. 'I'm getting changed.'

'No!' He leapt up behind her and this time there was nothing gentle in his hold as he halted her progress, turning her to face him. 'I want everyone to know you are my bride and that this is our wedding night.' His eyes lingered on hers, their dark secret depths rich and thick. 'And I want everyone to know exactly what we will be doing later.'

She looked down at his hand on her arm, his golden olive skin almost glowing against her own flesh in this lighting, before lifting her gaze to his eyes. 'That's some kind of sick.'

'No. That's some kind of pride. Every man will envy me. And I want them all to know you're mine. And that tonight I will have you.'

She swallowed. 'You're kidding yourself if you think that. You don't *have* anyone merely because of one simple act.' But, even as she spoke the words, she knew that sex with Diablo would never be simple. It would be as intense as his eyes—highly charged, like that kiss at the wedding that had been no mere meeting of lips but more a bolt of electricity.

'Come now, Briar,' he soothed, urging her down the stairs. 'Nobody said anything about having you only once. I do hope you enjoyed your meal. You're going to need the stamina.'

'Whatever for?' she questioned, feeling amazed they could be so openly bantering such a topic. 'I assumed you were man enough to take care of everything.'

He drew her closer to him, a smile tugging at his lips. 'I can see I'm going to enjoy tonight immensely.'

'At least that makes one of us.'

His eyes swirled with something that looked like challenge and for a moment she half expected him to argue the point. Instead he repeated just one word.

'Immensely.'

If she'd expected to be paraded through airports in her

wedding dress she was wrong. Shortly after they'd said their goodbyes and left the reception in Diablo's red TVR Tuscan sports car, it was clear that they were heading in the wrong direction for the airport. But it didn't matter where they were going really; she knew all too well what was waiting for her when they got there—Diablo had made that more than crystal clear.

For now she was content to settle back into the prestige convertible's black leather seats, enjoying the throaty purr of the engine as it ate up the miles. Heads turned around them as the car snarled its way north up the motorway, powering through the curves with fail-safe security.

It made sense that Diablo would possess a car like this—all lean lines and rumbling power, making toast of everything else on the road. The devil's car—red and racing, its curved bonnet suggestive of the three prongs of a pitchfork, with the devil himself behind the wheel.

'You're very quiet,' he said when they'd been travelling for half an hour, the lights of the city now way behind.

'I was thinking about your car,' she said.

'Oh?' Clearly, she'd surprised him. 'Tell me.'

'I was thinking how very like you it is.'

'You don't like my car?'

She resisted the urge to laugh. He almost sounded wounded. But of course he'd make that connection.

'I mean it's very stylish and powerful and...'

He looked at her. 'And?'

She'd been going to say *wicked*, but somehow that sounded too playful and there was nothing playful about Diablo. And she dared not say *dangerous*. That would be admitting way too much.

'And powerful.'

He surveyed her for a second or two till he returned his eyes to the road. 'You already said that.'

'Did I?' she asked ingenuously, closing down the conversation by pretending interest in the dark shrouded view outside her window and trying to forget the heated prickle his eyes had burned into her skin.

Some time later she must have dozed. She came to as he pulled off the main road, making his way coastward. The lights of a small seaside town beckoned but he turned off before then to a large property on a headland overlooking the ocean.

Electronic gates opened slowly in response to Diablo hitting a button on a remote and low lighting welcomed their approach up a long driveway.

'We're here?' she asked as they pulled up outside the imposing front doors of a house that seemed to go forever, its style reminiscent of a rambling hacienda.

He turned off the engine. 'We're here.'

'Where are we exactly?'

'A place called El Paradiso, about four hours north of Sydney.'

That far? She'd more than dozed; she'd slept most of the trip away.

'Come inside,' he said. 'I'll give you the tour.'

She lifted her long skirts and let him lead her up the steps to the entrance. She'd do the tour; she'd welcome it. Anything to delay the inevitable. The inevitable that stared her in the face when they concluded the tour more than a score of spacious rooms later in the biggest bedroom she'd ever seen.

A wall of windows spanned one side, the view over the dark sea even now breathtaking, the line of surf as waves crashed into the shore turned electric-blue under the full moon's power.

But it was hardly the view that snagged her attention and turned her mouth ashen dry. It was the bed. *Their bed.* An ocean wide itself, it held pride of place opposite the wall of glass, mocking her, reminding her of exactly why she was here.

Diablo crossed the room, slid a bolt and opened a door to a

deck that stretched out seawards. Avoiding the bed, she followed, breathing in the fresh air like a salve.

'Make yourself comfortable,' he said. 'I'll get the bags and something to drink.'

'I'm surprised you don't have a cast of thousands to run and fetch for you in a place this size.'

His eyelids slid half closed. 'I think I'm capable of moving a couple of bags. But as to staff, there's Joe and Luisa, a husband and wife team who maintain the house and gardens, who have their own detached accommodation close by. Luisa acts as housekeeper and cook when I'm here. I'll introduce you tomorrow.'

It was cool on the balcony, probably too cool, but tonight she didn't care, the air from the sea refreshing against her face, blowing away the last of her travel weariness. It might have been relaxing too, in other circumstances. But not tonight, not with what she knew was going to happen next. Despite the chill in the night air, she wasn't ready to go inside and face that bed.

And yet, even now her body seemed to be preparing itself, her skin tingling, her senses humming, on alert. Soon he would be back and then he would expect her to climb into that enormous expanse of bed and he would make love to her.

No!

He would have sex with her. Making love didn't come into it. He wanted children and she was no more than his brood mare. He'd no better than bought her and now he planned to drive her as ruthlessly as he drove his car. He would make her perform. He would use her like another of his possessions.

Or so he thought. She was here now and legally she was his wife. But be damned if she'd play incubator for his spawn, regardless of the terms of the contract they'd signed. She didn't even feel guilty about the arrangements she'd made to ensure that could never happen. A judge would never find her guilty for not wanting to bring a child into existence under these circumstances.

He studied her as she stood out there on the balcony looking out to sea, her long gown rippling in the soft breeze and glowing like shifting pearls under the moonlight, tendrils of her hair tumbling loose from the sleek coil at her head, their ends kissing that long sweep of neck. She looked like an ancient goddess, borne of the moon and made for loving. And soon he would be kissing that long sweep of neck, and places far beyond.

It was time.

He adjusted the interior lamps down to low before he joined her on the balcony, holding two flutes of champagne. She started at his approach, a tightening between her brows giving way to a tell-tale flutter at her throat and a panicked flaring of her eyes, betraying her otherwise cool façade.

'Champagne?' he offered. 'To calm your nerves.'

'Who said I'm nervous?' she asked as she took the glass.

'These,' he said, touching a hand alongside her eyes, 'and—' he moved to touch the pads of his fingers to that place on her throat where her pulse was still throwing out a frantic beat '—here.'

She stiffened and pulled away from his touch, retreating to the balustrade. He let her go, watching her as she took a sip from her glass.

She hugged her arms around herself, her shoulders tight. 'Are you cold out here?' he asked. 'Do you want to go inside?'

'No!' She blurted the word out before he'd hardly finished the question. 'I mean, it's not too cold. Just refreshing.' She took another sip of her champagne, as if to prove how relaxed she was, instead of the obvious bundle of nerves she was trying to contain.

'It's so beautiful here,' she said, looking over the lights of the town below, hugging the shoreline.

'You are,' he agreed. 'You look like a goddess in that gown.'

She raised her chin defiantly. 'You told me you wanted other men to see me, to know I was yours. But we saw no one.'

'And if I'd told you I wanted you to wear that gown because you look like a fairy tale princess, would you have believed me?'

She turned back to face the sea.

'I don't believe in fairy tales.'

'Who does?' he replied, joining her at the balustrade. 'But there are certain elements that appeal.'

'What, like happily ever after?' She gave a low laugh. *Not in this case.* 'I don't think so.'

'No,' he said emphatically. 'That concept belongs exclusively in fairy tales.'

She turned to look at him, her surprise giving way to cynicism. So he was bitter and jaded? So much the better. If he felt that way, it suited her purposes perfectly. Given his cynicism, he could hardly be surprised when she walked out of this marriage at the first chance she had.

She took another sip of her champagne, already thinking ahead to when she would be free again. 'At least we have that much in common,' she mused.

He looked at her and her half drained glass, his fathomless eyes suddenly speaking volumes. 'Maybe it's time to find out what else we have in common.'

Anticipation flowed through her in a rush. But she wasn't ready. 'A generous lover', he'd described himself as. Would she find that to be true? She didn't want to. She wanted reasons to hate him instead. So, instead of answering, she turned back against the balustrade, looking out to the sea.

'What is this place?' she asked as if he'd never spoken. 'Did you build it? It looks like something straight from a Spanish movie set.'

He recognised the change of topic for the avoidance technique it was, but he'd play along for a minute if it relaxed her. No longer than that, though. Already his body was tightening, its expectations for the night to come too acute to ignore. 'I built it for my mother.'

She turned her head. 'What happened to her? I know next to nothing of your family. You've never mentioned a thing about any of them.'

He shrugged. 'It's not important.'

'Of course it's important. You expect me to sleep with you, but I don't know the first thing about who you really are. You might as well be a stranger.'

'Strangers sleep together all the time.'

Briar stiffened. 'Not this little black duck.'

'So my new wife didn't spend her university days sleeping around? So much the better.' He had no doubt he'd soon obliterate her memories of each and every one of her former lovers but the last thing he wanted was her former boyfriends crawling out of the woodwork.

Her head spun around, her amber eyes sparking like shooting stars in the moonlight. 'If you say so,' she bit back, 'but surely it must have occurred to you that I might just have spent my university days sleeping around with all the people I *did* know.'

He downed the balance of champagne in his flute in an instant, flinging it sideways to shatter into a thousand crystal shards on the far side of the balcony. 'Then what is to come will hardly be a surprise to you. I can't see the point of delaying any longer.'

She crossed her arms defiantly. 'If that's your idea of foreplay, I'd suggest you borrow a couple of books from your local library.'

In a sudden and unexpected movement he'd trapped her against the railing, imprisoning her with his arms, his body so hard against the balusters she had to unlock her arms and throw them back to steady herself.

'Something you're about to find out, my lovely wife,' he crooned as he dipped his lips to the place where her pulse jumped erratically in her throat. 'I wrote those books.'

Talk about bloody-minded arrogance! She was just about to tell him how egotistical he sounded when his tongue touched the flesh of her throat, searing her skin and damn near cauterising her words dead. Flames radiated outwards from the path his tongue was taking like a rolling tide of desire. Her breasts firmed, her nipples aching and heat pooled low down inside her. And suddenly, the way his tongue had been unleashed on her throat, she didn't doubt his claims. If he could wreak such havoc by merely touching his mouth to her neck...

Just then he lifted his head, found her mouth and transferred his magic there, his lips insistent but gentle, coaxing, encouraging. And behind it all she could taste his hunger—hunger for *her*—and resolve took a back seat and she found herself kissing him back, joining in the sensual dance of lips and mouth and tongue.

It should have been easy to resist him, to push him away, but the feelings he was unleashing inside her and the warm tingling rush of preparedness stripped down her defences. She didn't want to feel this way about Diablo! She didn't want her body to respond to someone who was so self-serving, who wasn't interested in her but for her name and her baby-bearing capabilities.

And yet her knees threatened to buckle, her spine weakening under the onslaught of his mouth and the press of his body against hers.

He lifted his head away from hers and she had to blink to clear her vision to focus on those dark eyes, almost black in this light, fully intent upon hers. But his brief absence gave her breathing space—vital breathing space—and she wasn't about to miss the opportunity to regain some kind of coolness between them. He might have the piece of paper that bound them legally together, but he had no rights over her heart and soul.

'I see,' she managed, pretending to be unmoved in a voice that sounded more like heavy breathing, while at the same time pushing against the barrier of his arms. 'In that case, I might as well go and get undressed in preparation for the main event.'

She attempted to edge out between him and the balustrade but he stopped her, one hand at her throat, his thumb gently stroking as he moved even closer. 'Oh, no, you don't,' he murmured, swinging her into his arms as easily as if she weighed nothing at all.

'Undressing you is *my* job.'

CHAPTER FIVE

DIABLO'S mouth arrested her gasp, cutting off any protest more effectively than if he'd argued the point, only this time the gentleness and sensuality of his kiss was gone, replaced by a ferocious sexuality so raw she could feel the impact to her core. He swung her into his arms as if she were weightless, moulding her to him, cradling her like a prize as he carried her inside, his mouth moving over hers with a fierceness that left her senses reeling and any protest abandoned.

She didn't have to hold him—there was no way he was about to drop her—but somehow it felt necessary to wind her arms around his neck and splay her fingers through his hair, and to graze her peaking breasts against his broad chest as she pulled herself closer to his mouth.

Diablo growled, deep in his throat, and the sound reverberated through her, sweeping to and fro like a hot tide that concentrated down to one pulsing point between her thighs.

Once inside he released her legs, letting her feet slowly slide down to the ground while his hands moulded her against him, length against length. He cupped her behind, forcing her to embrace with her body the solid column of his erection.

He was so big, so alive, the sheer force of his hardness a fascinating thing—*a terrifying thing*. To imagine that somehow she

might take that length inside her… Fear jagged through her—
and if she couldn't?

Wouldn't that be too funny? What a way that would be for
Diablo to realise he'd chosen the wrong woman for his needs.
And then he slid her shoestring straps over her shoulders and
peeled her bodice away, releasing her swollen breasts into his
hands, and a feeling akin to insanity told her it would be *she* who
would be the loser.

How could she ever have imagined she could resist him? As
soon as he touched her, she was on fire for him.

He leaned down and took one pebbled peak between his lips,
flicking the tip of it with his tongue, and need crashed through her.
Her back arched involuntarily, pushing her breasts towards him like
an invitation. He accepted, filling his mouth with her aching flesh,
circling her nipple with his tongue, scraping his teeth evocatively
over her skin while he rolled her other nipple between his fingers.

She held on to him, clutching his head and shoulders, knowing
that if she didn't she would collapse, right here and now, on the
floor. Her fingers tracked through his hair, his ponytail tie pulled
out by her fingers, his thick collar-length black hair a silken
curtain on her hands.

He lifted his head from her breast and she twisted her hands
in his hair in desperation but he only turned to her other breast,
lavishing on that nipple the same devout attention, worshipping
her flesh with his mouth.

There was slight pressure behind her and then the long sensual
glide of her zip. His hands slid under the fabric, sweeping away
the sides, turning her spine molten as finally he lifted his head
and let her gown glide, a silken waterfall, to the floor.

Eyes, at once wild and desperate, regarded her in a hot display
of need, taking in her peaked breasts, her tiny scrap of underwear
and the lace-topped stockings. He dragged in a breath so hard
she felt the rush of air.

'*Dios*,' he rasped, 'but you are beautiful.'

Her own breathing was just as out of control. Fast and shallow, she felt light-headed and faint and never more in need all at the same time. He seemed to sense her condition and in an instant he'd swept her out of the circle of her gown and laid her reverently on the bed.

'So beautiful,' he growled as he wrenched off his jacket and shirt and threw them into the corner. Her eyes widened at the satin perfection of his olive skin, the play of light and shadow over the muscled walls of his chest. She ached to touch him there and to run her hands over that perfect surface, to where his tight waist disappeared into the waistband of his trousers—the waistband he was now unbuttoning.

His shoes and socks had gone while her eyes were elsewhere and now his trousers joined them. Her mouth went dry as his silken briefs outlined the burgeoning force beneath, bucking with its own life force. Oh, what was she doing? She was such a fraud. She couldn't do this!

And then he eased his underwear over and down and her mind went blank. He joined her on the bed, collecting her into his arms, and with trepidation tempered with relief she joined willingly in his kiss as his hands swept her curves, tracking over her super-charged flesh in an erotic dance.

Every part of her seemed on fire. Every part of her came alive as he followed the trail of his touch with his mouth. Once again he suckled her breasts and this time she was grateful she was lying down. She was past standing, past holding herself together. His fingers traced down her legs and up again, driving her crazy with both their proximity and their distance to that aching core, but when his hand lingered over her mound she tensed.

'Diablo,' she pleaded.

'I know,' he murmured as his tongue lazily snaked around her nipple.

But he didn't know. He couldn't. And when his hands had worked away her damp underwear and his fingers dipped lower, separating her and exploring her innermost flesh, circling one tight bud, she was too far gone to explain.

'So ready,' he murmured, 'so slick.'

And, as if to prove a point, he slid one finger deep inside. She gasped at the intimate intrusion at the same time that he groaned, a desperate kind of sound that he followed with a rush of words and action.

'And so tight!'

He lunged up the bed, positioning himself between her legs, nudging himself against her slick core.

'Diablo!' she cried as the pressure mounted below—unfamiliar pressure, pushing against flesh untested, unproven.

'So tight,' he repeated as he pushed through her final barrier in one long fluid lunge.

She tensed, expecting pain, but there was none. Only pressure, a feeling of fullness that stretched and filled her inside in a way she'd never dreamed possible.

His eyes sought hers, as if he sensed something wrong, even as he pulled slowly out of her. *Could he tell?* She felt her muscles contract around him, not wanting to let him go, but then he lunged into her again, and then again.

She followed his lead, the rhythm beating furiously between them, the tide rising, carrying her higher and higher up the shore, while his dark eyes continued to stare down at her, the beads of sweat on his forehead proclaiming both his effort and his control.

She held his eyes while she matched his movements, tilting her hips towards him, letting the tide sweep her up with his next deep thrust, until she couldn't hold his gaze any longer. Her head thrashed from side to side as he slammed into her, the tide lifting her one last time before it smashed her against the cliff face in an explosion of starlit sea foam.

He crashed right behind her, his body tensing before his final shuddering release, collapsing alongside her, bringing her still joined with him.

They lay together, their breathing slowly easing, their bodies spent. So that was sex, she mused, knowing it was better than she'd ever imagined possible. And if that was sex with someone you detested, what must it feel like to actually make love with someone you cared about?

She turned her head sideways, watched his face, his eyes closed, his breathing now slow and even as if he was sleeping. Now would be a good time to get out from under his arm and find something to cover her up.

She made a move to ease herself away but his arm tightened over her, preventing her escape. 'No,' he said, his eyes opening to reveal dark thunder as he raised himself up on one elbow over her.

'Why didn't you tell me you were a virgin?'

Silence stretched out between them, strained within a millimetre of breaking-point. So he had realised. But what did it matter? Was he now going to pretend contrition? He'd wanted her in his bed and he'd got what he'd wanted.

She swallowed, still feeling suddenly shy and nervous and exposed. 'How did you know?'

'Did you think you could hide the truth from me?'

She shrugged and turned her head away. 'I should have realised such a hot-shot lover would recognise a total novice in an instant.'

'Did I hurt you?'

'What do you care?'

'You should have told me.'

'Why? What the hell difference would it have made? Am I to suddenly believe you care how I feel? Not likely.'

His eyes hardened, their surface reflecting a play of light and dark like some shiny glinting stone.

'What does it matter? It matters because it means your father is a worse businessman than even I gave him credit for.'

'What are you talking about?'

'I would have settled upon him twice the amount if I'd known you were a virgin.'

'You bastard!' She pushed at his shoulders and attempted to wrench her leg out from under him at the same time. 'You can't buy and sell people like just one more of your precious properties. It doesn't work that way.'

'No?' he questioned, making a mockery of her attempts to escape. 'Well, it sure got me you, and...' He pressed himself to her side and, with a small cry of shock, she felt him hardening against her. 'It got me you, right where I want you to be.'

'You disgust me!' she said, trying desperately to edge away even as the knowledge he was hard again and wanting her caused her flesh to tingle once more in preparation.

'Do I?' he challenged, jamming her free arm back against the pillows, covering her mouth with a crushing kiss that took her breath away with its ruthless ferocity, so punishing was its intensity.

'Do I really disgust you?' he demanded, when finally he withdrew from the kiss, his lips hovering bare millimetres above hers. 'That's not the impression you gave me earlier.'

'So I was keen to be rid of my virginity at last. Don't fancy yourself—I had to throw it away on someone! You just happened to be the only one around.'

With a twist of his body he'd insinuated one knee between her legs, his body now hovering over her like a thundercloud.

'And I could have sworn you enjoyed every minute of it.' The words were squeezed out of a grimace chiselled from a granite-lined face.

'Sorry to disappoint you.'

'Really? So I didn't just make you come?'

She glared up at him. 'I was faking it.'

His eyes turned suddenly feral, glistening, and instantly she could see he'd taken her blatant lie for a challenge.

'Then how about I give you a chance to "fake it" again?'

'Diablo!' she cried, but he'd already positioned himself, his intentions clear. Immediately she regretted her foolish words, afraid of being swept away by the maelstrom this man conjured up in, but already he was nudging against that sensitive flesh, testing her newfound muscles as he pressed himself home, and her protest turned into a gasp as she received him, her back arching as he drew one peaked nipple into his hot wet mouth.

He drove into her, almost to the hilt, before withdrawing in a rush that had her gasping all over again with the sudden loss.

'You don't enjoy this?' he growled roughly against the flesh of her breast, his voice thick before his tongue curled once more around her nipple.

Then he drove into her again, this time deeper, withdrawing again only to power himself home once more.

'Or this?'

Spears of current coursed through her, forming an inner circuitry from her breasts to the muscles framing him, stretched and tight. It was impossible not to like it. It was just as impossible to utter more than a breath of appreciation every time he filled her.

His eyes glittered above her as slowly he built up the speed, burying himself ever deeper, ramping up the power, crashing and thundering into her like a storm front. And obviously satisfied she was faking nothing, he returned his attention to her breasts, tugging at her nipples with his teeth, filling his mouth with her aching flesh, every flick of his tongue lashing at her defences, every nip of his teeth drawing her further into the turbulence.

So she clung to him, going with him, fearful that if she let go she'd be spun and tossed away. She anchored herself against him, caught up in the raw energy he was unleashing in them both, reducing her entire world to this one intense whirlpool.

And when she came it was at the height of the storm, with a thunderclap like a roar from the gods splitting the heavens asunder, and she was thrown into the darkness, fractured and broken and spent, while the waves of shuddering slowly abated, rolling through her like thunder disappearing rumbling away into the distance.

Precipitation coated her cheeks in the storm's wake as she realised what she'd done. Once again she'd let her body betray her. Once again she'd let herself be carried away in passion by Diablo. She rolled herself away, taking advantage of his momentary inertia, swiping at his too-late grabbing attempt to stop her.

'Let me go,' she insisted on a sob, turning her head away so he wouldn't see the tracks of her tears as she bolted from the bed.

'Still faking it?' he called out behind her, his words a steely accusation.

'I'd say you made your point perfectly, wouldn't you?'

She snatched up her handbag on the way to the *en suite* bathroom, locking the door behind her before dragging on a robe hanging at the back of the door. It was way too big but right now she just needed something gentle against her skin, something warm and comforting after the cold fire that was Diablo. Then she dived into her bag, desperately burrowing through the contents until she found what she was looking for. She popped the bubble and pushed out the tiny pill into the palm of her hand.

The door handle rattled behind her. 'Briar!' he called. 'Are you all right?'

'You expect me to believe you care?'

'Let me in.'

'Go to hell!' she yelled. *Back where you belong.* The door rattled one more time before she heard a muttered curse and the sound of his irate footsteps receding across the jarrah floorboards. She took a deep breath as she turned back, shocking herself when she caught sight of her reflection in the mirror. Some time during the action her hair had fallen free of restraint to float wildly around her shoulders, her lips looked pink and tender, their edges smudged and ill-defined, and her eyes stared back at her, wide and lost. Some time tonight, maybe the moment he'd swept her up in his arms, she'd lost herself. She'd lost her way. She'd clung to him, wanting him to take her higher, wanting him to love her, even when she knew she shouldn't.

Tears slid silently down her cheeks. So much for her resistance. It had crumbled with one touch of his mouth. And the shame of it was that he could do it all again just as easily. Now she had but one defence.

She threw her hand to her mouth and swallowed the pill down, chasing it with a scoop of water from the tap, before stashing the pills back in her bag and zipping them down tight.

Because, damn him to hell and back, she might have to endure his passion and his bed, but she would *never* bear his child!

Diablo paced the room like a caged lion, eating up the metres of polished floorboards between each wall as if it was a shoebox rather than the massive suite that it was.

Why the hell hadn't she told him? He'd never suspected she was a virgin—she'd never so much as hinted—but then, when he'd driven into her, experiencing her impossibly sweet tightness, he'd wondered. She hadn't cried out but she'd tensed suddenly around him like a vice, her eyes wide open and startled like a doe's, and the half formed question in his mind had turned to suspicion.

But he still hadn't been sure, not totally, until she'd confirmed it with her quiet affirmation.

'How did you know?'

She'd admitted everything with those four simple words. He

paused before the sliding doors, looking out at the dark sea as it shifted, its surface glistening in the moonlight.

Dios! Why hadn't she alerted him? And then, damn her, why had she acted as if it hadn't mattered? As if it was nothing special?

He was pleased there had been no other lovers. Relieved. And yet he had rewarded her virtue by taking her roughly, *cruelly*, not once, but twice, the second time even *after* he knew how inexperienced she was.

This was no way to introduce a woman into the ways of the bedroom. She could be a willing pupil too, if he took his time, if he showed her what was possible, instead of acting like a monster in her bed. And he wanted her to learn. For her first time she'd been amazingly responsive—*no wonder he'd been uncertain*—her body melding with his, moving with his rhythm, matching it and meeting his rise and fall as if she was born to it. And when she'd come apart in his arms it had been real, for them both. No wonder he'd been so keen to take her again so quickly.

His body stirred, his blood quickening and collecting as he recalled her sweet curves, her deliciously smooth skin that felt like silk and tasted like honey. Oh, yes, he'd make amends by showing her how it could be between a man and a woman.

But not tonight. He looked down at himself and cursed. After what had happened before, the last thing she needed was to see him like this. And he didn't want her on guard, he didn't need her any more scared. He wanted her receptive and warm and eager. But if he saw her emerge from the bathroom now, all fresh-skinned and gleaming and dressed in little more than a towel, then he wouldn't be going soft any time soon.

Damn! What he needed right now was a different kind of exercise. He needed laps. Mind-numbing, body-punishing, repetitive laps.

He turned his back on both the view of the shimmering sea

and the promise of the glittering jewel that lay behind the door to the *en suite* bathroom and headed for the indoor pool.

He was gone. The dimly lit room wore his absence like a vacuum, expanding to twice the size without his aura to eat up the space. Briar let go a breath she'd been holding and pushed herself away from the door frame. She'd been braced for…what? Another confrontation? Another battle leading to sex? Whatever it was, she was relieved he had taken himself away some time while she'd stood under the shower and tried to scour all trace of his touch from her skin.

Not that it had worked. Her skin might be relieved of a layer or two of cells but what chance did mere soap have in eradicating the memories of the fires he'd lit under the surface? Even now her skin prickled with newly discovered sensations at the memories.

I hate him, she told herself, while she hated herself even more for the strange sexual fascination he'd awakened within her. Never before had she experienced such earth-shattering sensations. She'd be lying if she pretended she hadn't liked it…if she pretended she didn't want more…

With a shiver she pushed herself away from the door and darted across the room to where he'd left her bag. A quick run through the contents turned to two and still no nightgown. But why was that not a surprise? She could just imagine him giving the command for someone to pack her bag *sans* night attire. Well blow him, she thought, diving under the rumpled covers without removing the robe. As defences went, it wasn't much, but she felt safer just hugging it around herself.

Where was Diablo, anyway? Already sick of her? Or still seething after her stinging insult to his manhood? He needn't be; he'd more than proved she wasn't immune to his charms.

For a long time she lay there, her eyes flying awake at the slightest noise, her ears straining for the sound of an approaching footfall, but all she heard was the rhythmic whoosh of the ocean as it slid endlessly up and down the shore below, gradually quietening as sleep came up to claim her.

He watched her while she slept, her eyes closed, her lashes meshed together, her lips slightly parted, while burnished copper laced hair spilled loose beneath her on the pillow. A picture of innocence. But then, not quite so innocent any more.

A swell of masculine pride overcame him. She was his now and his alone. Nobody had had her before him. Nobody would again. Nobody but him.

It was enough to make him hard again, despite still feeling the effects of his ten kilometre swim. He shook his head as he eased himself into bed alongside her. He had chosen well indeed when he had decided on Briar Davenport for the mother of his children.

CHAPTER SIX

WARMTH enveloped Briar like a drug, holding her hostage to sleep, even as the lightening sky told her it must be morning. But it wasn't the sunlight infiltrating the curtains at the window that made her snap her eyes open, but the sudden understanding of the source of her comfort.

Diablo's body curved around hers, one arm thrown casually over her hip, a hip that nestled in dangerous proximity to another more carnal source of heat. She tensed and immediately regretted it. For even the tiniest movement meant friction between his naked body and the robe she still had tightly wound around her.

He shifted in his sleep, his hard length grazing her while his hand drifted north to come to rest at the under-swell of her breast. Oh, Lord, if even his unintentional touch through a layer of towelling sent sparks shimmying through her, then how much more so would it be when he woke and expected to make love to her? Already her breasts felt tight and full, her nipples at attention, longing for his hand to slip further around and tighten over them. Already flesh so tender it should ache for days seemed to tingle back into life.

How could it be so?

After last night she should hate him more than ever, but what her mind told her and what her body craved seemed to be two different things. Diablo had thrown a switch inside her that had her body wilfully ignoring her head.

Behind her Diablo stirred again and she held her breath. His arm dropped to her hip again and tightened, pulling her hard against his erection as he raised himself on one elbow and dropped his lips to her cheek.

'Good morning, Mrs Barrentes,' he growled in that way that rumbled right through to her core.

'Morning,' she replied thinly, on tenterhooks, waiting for him—*expecting him*—to push her robe away and take her right then and there.

Already her blood had thickened to a crawl, her breathing similarly hindered as she anticipated what was to follow.

Then his hand disappeared with a lurch of the bed and he launched himself from the other side. Anticipation turned to an unexpectedly bitter stab of disappointment.

'What would you like to do today?' he asked, padding across the floor to slide the door to the balcony open, seemingly unconcerned by his nakedness and his lingering erection as he breathed in the new day. She studied him, standing there. If she hadn't realised it last night, the cold light of morning told her just how perfect a male specimen her new husband was. His body was sculpted perfection, from his broad shoulders down to the muscled wall of his chest and tapering to those lean and powerful hips. The view from the back lacked nothing either—the dimples either side of his spine where his waist was most narrow and, further down, the tight symmetry of his behind. She forced her eyes away. She shouldn't stare.

Because she didn't care what he looked like, not really. It was just that she'd never had the opportunity to study the male animal in such detail before.

'Would you like to visit some local galleries?' he asked over his shoulder, not waiting for an answer. 'Or take a walk along the beach to the town?'

Confusion muddied her thoughts. For a man who last night had been as hungry as a wolf, and who looked ready to go another three rounds right now, the noticeable absence of a continuing-where-he-left-off-last-night option on that list of suggestions was damning. And no, not even the renowned Diablo Barrentes could believe himself so virile that his work was done and that she was pregnant already.

She pushed herself up in the bed. Was he already tired of her? She'd been sampled and found wanting, too inexperienced, too argumentative. He was no doubt more conversant with a more amenable lover. *All of which helped her case*, she realised with a jolt. If she didn't breed, which she most certainly wouldn't, then this crazy marriage wouldn't last a year, let alone two.

And wasn't that just what she wanted?

So where was the sweet whiff of satisfaction that should have accompanied that thought? Damn, but it was irritating. Just like him parading around in the buff was irritating.

'Don't you have a robe you can put on or something?'

He turned towards her, his lips raised in a smile. 'Does my body bother you?'

'Of course not,' she lied, feeling suddenly too hot and uncomfortable in bed. 'I just thought you might be cold.'

'Do I look cold to you?' He turned fully side on to her so there was no way she could miss his meaning.

Hell, no! Even half erect he looked hot enough to set the sheets ablaze if he came anywhere near them. She blinked and tried—unsuccessfully—to drag her eyes away, fascinated as he pulsed and grew.

'I wouldn't know,' she lied again through a mouth so suddenly dry it was like talking through a layer of ash.

He raised one eyebrow and moved closer to the bed, with a fluid stealth to his steps like a jungle cat closing in on a kill, the look in his eyes dark and turbulent.

This is it, she realised as she pushed herself back against the bed head, her pulse racing as she watched him draw closer, anticipation curling and unfurling in her gut. *At last...*

He leaned over, placing his two hands on to the bedcover either side of her, pinning her down.

'Besides which...' he whispered as he reached one hand up behind her neck, causing her breath to hitch as her world slowed down to a crawl. His fingers caressed her neck, a sensual massage of fingertips and thumb. His lips slow danced a bare millimetre from her own. Already she could taste their welcoming warmth, already she could feel their fluid glide over her own. Then, without warning, his hand dropped to her collar and he tugged on it twice. '...you're wearing my robe.'

It took a moment for his words to register. Especially when she was still too busy looking forward to the meshing of his lips with hers.

But in the space of a blink his eyes had gone from fiery intent to mocking, the sensual slash of his lips now tilted up in amusement, and she realised she'd just been played for a prize fool.

Bile rose in her throat. He'd never intended to make love to her. It had never been on his agenda this morning at all. And yet she'd practically rolled over for him, the man she was supposed to hate. *Did hate.* Especially now. Diablo inspired hate like an art form.

She scooted to the far side of the bed and threw back the covers, collecting the voluminous folds of the robe around her before brushing her hair back from her face.

'Sorry. I won't make the same mistake again. It just seems that nobody thought to pack me any pyjamas or a robe.'

He stood, the look in his eyes inscrutable. 'Maybe because *"nobody"* thought you'd need them.'

'Then nobody was wrong.'

His eyes regarded her coolly. 'There's no need for prudishness now. You are my wife and you have a beautiful body. It's no crime to display it.'

'And if I don't wish to display it?'

After a moment's hesitation he just shrugged. 'Have a shower. I'll get breakfast and coffee organised. I think we'll have it on the terrace. Then I'll take you for a drive. It might relax you.'

'You think? With you along it would have to be one hell of a drive.'

His chest rose on a mighty breath, his nostrils flaring. 'I'll see you on the terrace,' he said at last, as he strode into the adjoining dressing room and slammed the door.

It was relaxing too, Briar thought, or maybe it was just the after-effects of the glass of wine with her bowl of spaghetti marinara. Whatever, it had been hours since they'd left the house, tense and silent, this morning, driving along the coast, streaking along the highway with the top down and the balmy wind in their hair. Together they'd checked out every small town for their galleries and coffee shops until finally they'd found a tiny Italian restaurant with a view out past the string of pine trees that fringed the shoreline to the grey-blue sea and had settled in for a late lunch.

The table had been cleared, their coffee brought and for the first time an easy peace seemed to settle over them. Diablo leaned back in his chair, his white knitted top stretching tight over his broad chest, the colour a bold contrast that only emphasised his olive skin and Spanish good looks.

She regarded his profile as he looked out to sea—the heavy slash of eyebrows, the strong line of nose, the autocratic chin. Not classically handsome by any means but certainly head-turning. In another century Diablo would have been a conquistador, a Spanish adventurer, intent on invasion and conquest. She took a sip of her latte. Funny how some things never changed.

His head swung around, his eyes capturing her frank appraisal and narrowing in response.

'You look deep in thought.'

She cradled the warm glass of latte between her hands, feeling suddenly caught out, glad to have something inanimate to suddenly focus her attention on.

'Why did they call you Diablo? Doesn't that mean devil in Spanish? It seems an odd name to give a baby.'

He smiled and leaned forward. 'You don't think it suits me?'

She replaced her coffee cup on its saucer and regarded him levelly. 'I'm just wondering how they got it so right.'

His smile broadened, suddenly taking his features beyond head-turning and into another attention-riveting league entirely.

'*Touché*. It's not a conventional baby name. But my mother was hardly conventional. And hers wasn't an easy pregnancy. I made her suffer so much she took to calling me *el diablo adentro*—the devil inside.' He shrugged. 'The name stuck.'

It was the most he'd ever told her about his family.

'What was your mother like?' she asked, her interest piqued.

He leaned back into his chair, linking his hands over his stomach, looking up at the ceiling. 'She was a strong woman, beautiful and passionate.'

Like mother, like son.

'And your father?'

'I never knew my father. He died before we came to Australia.' His voice was flat, bleak. And, while his eyes were fixed on the ceiling above, it was clear his focus was elsewhere.

'It must have been so difficult for your mother to move from Spain to Australia under such circumstances. Why did she do it?'

'She had no choice. And it wasn't Spain, but Chile.'

'I thought you were Spanish.'

'Yes, Castilian. My parents' families came from a region near Madrid. But my grandparents opposed their marriage—they were both very young and their families were very rich with their own ideas as to their children's future—so they left everything behind and ran away together.'

'But why Chile? Surely at that time it wasn't safe.'

His mouth tightened. 'They knew it wasn't safe, but they were principled. My father had studied medicine and was in demand by the aid agencies, and they saw the chance to work together to help people rather than live in comfort at home but apart. Two years later my father was killed in an attack on their hospital, my mother narrowly escaping, only then realising she was pregnant. She wanted to continue my father's work but I made her too sick to help anyone and then the situation became too dangerous. She fled.'

'She couldn't go home to Spain?'

'Her family had disowned her. She had defied them. They wanted nothing to do with her.'

'Oh, God.' She could barely imagine the suffering his mother had been through, or the pain. And then the bitterness when her family had turned their backs on her in her hour of need—pregnant with their grandchild and still they had wanted nothing more to do with her. It was too horrible. 'How did she ever cope?'

'She worked,' he continued. 'She cleaned, she cooked. She washed and ironed—all her life she battled to bring me up.'

'She must have been so proud of you.'

He looked sharply across at her, a frown drawing his thick dark brows even closer together. Then he lifted his cup to his lips, finishing the rest of his coffee in one swallow. 'It's time we were moving on,' he told her as he stood up to go.

Two and a half hours and a dozen tiny tourist havens later, Diablo turned the car for home.

Briar pushed herself back in the plush leather upholstery. He'd been so different today from the Diablo she was used to.

He'd been charming, the perfect companion as they'd explored shop after shop and she'd surprised herself by actually enjoying his company. And now she knew more about his family than ever before. How that must have shaped him—never knowing his father, being raised by a mother who'd lost everything, including the love of her life, and who had been reduced to refugee status. And, after all that, she'd had to slog her guts out to provide for her son.

Was it any wonder he was driven to succeed? He'd built his mother that house overlooking the sea. He'd given her back something of what she'd lost. Before today, she wouldn't have thought him capable of thinking about anyone but himself.

She slid a glance sideways in his direction, taking in his strong profile. Which one was the real Diablo—the ruthless businessman who undercut the competitor's position until their business collapsed or the charming, flashing-eyed Continental with the heartrending heritage?

He turned his head, capturing her gaze, his dark eyes hidden by his wraparound sunglasses. But they didn't disguise the shift in his brow as he frowned.

'Tired?' he asked, before turning his attention back to the road.

'A little,' she replied honestly.

'Maybe a quiet night is in order.'

His words and his voice stroked her like a caress. But it was the look he followed it with that struck her, melting her bones so that her body sank deeper into the upholstery. 'Or at least,' he added, his look full of meaning, 'an early one.'

His words seemed to smoulder between them. Last night hadn't been quiet, the chemistry between them explosive, the electricity sparking. She swallowed, dry-mouthed, the moisture in her body gravitating south. Was she ready to go another round with Diablo? Her body seemed to think so.

But she'd been ready this morning too, when she'd thought

he was similarly coming on to her, only to have him reject her cold. It hadn't been because he wasn't aroused—there was no way a man that erect wasn't aroused. But after his sensual provocation—his lean, stealthy walk towards her, his pinning her to the bed—after all that, his calculated withdrawal had been like a slap in the face.

Was that what he was doing now—building her up only to smash her down again? Undermining her confidence and her new-found sexuality as effectively as he'd undercut every one of the Davenport business interests, toying with her father's defences until he was ultimately ruined.

She couldn't let that happen to her again. Just as she should never let herself be swayed by his sad stories. This was the same man who had coldly destroyed her father's business. He'd damned near destroyed all of their lives. How could she so easily dismiss what he'd done simply because he knew how to make her feel like a woman?

No, she had to keep what he'd done in the forefront of her mind and ensure she kept a tight lid on her body's reactions. Diablo Barrentes would not possess her. She wouldn't let him.

With a newly reclaimed backbone, she straightened in her seat, directing her attention outside the car.

'Whatever.'

He dragged in a breath and checked the oncoming lane before accelerating in a roar of power past the stream of vehicles ahead, leaving them almost dawdling in their wake.

She wanted him—he could tell. All day long he'd been breaking down the barriers between them, warming her to him, and it had been working. He'd even surprised himself by telling her more about his family than he'd ever told another living soul. And she'd listened, as if she cared, as if it mattered to someone else other than him. But then the golden shutters had come down in her eyes and closed her off to him again.

Damn! His body ached to join with her again. He could have had her this morning too, if he'd wanted. Even huddled behind the covers he had seen she'd just about been begging for it and, *dios*, he'd been more than tempted. But he'd still been too angry—with her for not telling him she'd been a virgin—with himself for making no allowances for it. And he didn't want to take her angry—not next time. He wanted to savour her, to take her slow and not in a heated rush.

Besides, she would enjoy it more when her muscles had time to recover from last night's onslaught. He registered the heated concentration of blood at the memories of entering that glorious body and cursed under his breath. If only he could convince his own body he was prepared to wait that long!

Another vehicle slowed their progress, seguing with his frustration, until the road ahead cleared and the Tuscan's acceleration once again came into its own. He loved how this car handled—its sleek lines, its throaty purr when it idled and its all out roar when he pushed it to the limits. It was almost like handling a woman, putting her through her paces, having her perform at his bidding.

So Briar liked to think she was different? She'd proven with her response to him last night that she wasn't *that* different. It wouldn't take long but she'd come around.

And, when she did, he'd drive her wild. So he would have to wait a bit longer? She would be worth the wait. No question.

The sky was already tinted with a reddish-gold sunset when twenty minutes later he pulled the car up alongside the house. She was out of the door and up the few steps to the porch before he had a chance to round the car and open it for her.

'Briar?'

She pulled off her sunglasses as she wheeled around, tension lining her eyes, her mouth tight as she looked down at him. 'I've got a headache. If you don't mind, I think I might just lie down for a while.'

A headache? The oldest excuse under the sun and she was aiming it at him?

He climbed the steps slowly. Decisively. 'That came on suddenly.' There'd certainly been no sign of it earlier, not until he'd made mention of having an early night. Since then she hadn't said a word, making the rest of their journey in stony silence.

Her eyes followed his ascent up the steps, until she was looking up at him. 'I'm tired. It's been a long couple of days.'

'And dinner?'

She shook her head. 'I don't want anything.'

'Suit yourself,' he said gruffly, reaching past her for the door handle. 'In that case I'll be in my office. I've got plenty of work to do.'

'I can imagine. All those corporate takeovers to manage must take some strategising.'

The snippy edge to her voice irritated him bone-deep and he straightened, pulling his hand away. 'It seems your headache doesn't make you too ill to want to stick your thorns into me.'

She laughed, a harsh, bitter sound. 'You don't even try to deny it.'

'Don't knock it, Briar. I'm a businessman and, without my business, your father wouldn't have the funds now to keep himself and your precious family home afloat. He and your family, yourself included, would have sunk into the gutter without trace.'

'Only because you'd already deposited us there in the first place! You destroyed his business, you stole his clients, you undercut prices till they were unsustainable and drove us into loss!'

'And that's all down to me? And why is it, then, that your father could not defend himself against me, a brash newcomer on the scene, and him a fourth generation businessman? Don't you think it seems unlikely, given his pedigree?'

'You know why. Everybody knows why.'

He tilted his head, moved a step closer, more than satisfied when she backed herself hard against the wall, her hands splayed flat against it. 'Maybe you should fill me in.'

Under the rays from the setting sun her eyes sparked gold fire, her full lips pouting with indignation and he could almost hear the machinations of her mind.

'All right. If you're so desperate to hear what everyone thinks about you. You've only got to where you are because you're ruthless and cruel and think nothing of grinding other people into the dirt beneath your feet. You'll stop at nothing to reach the top, no matter who you hurt along the way, no matter what the cost.'

Her chest was heaving, her colour high, and he was content to drink in her passion and her intensity while she battled to steady her breathing. She was beautiful when she was angry, her eyes alight with challenge, clearly anticipating some kind of fiery response. He smiled. He wasn't about to give her one.

He placed one hand on the wall beside her head and leaned closer, watching her eyes widen when he trailed the fingertips of his other hand down the side of her face.

'And this is a problem because…?'

Her chest rose on a gasp and she turned her head away from him. 'I don't believe you! You're actually proud of your reputation.'

'And you would believe me if I tried to defend myself?'

'Not a chance!'

He shrugged and took her chin between his thumb and forefinger, tilting her face up to his. 'Then why should I bother? You've already made up your mind about me. I'm cruel and ruthless, you say, then so be it. I would hate to disappoint you, my prickly wild rose.'

'I am not your wild rose!' she insisted, trying unsuccessfully to shrug her chin out of his grip. 'I am not your *anything*!'

He tugged her chin higher, leaning in towards her—so close

he could feel her own sweet scent weave its web around him, so close he could taste her heat. 'You are my wife.'

'Only because a lousy piece of paper says so.'

'No! Because you are my woman!'

His mouth cut short her protest, her already parted lips making his quest even easier, giving him access to pillage her mouth, to drink from her sweetness, to feed and build a hunger he felt like a wild animal raging inside him.

One hand tangled in her hair, angling her head closer, releasing the pin at the nape of her head and sending her hair spilling over his forearm like a silken wash.

Dios, but he'd been waiting for this all day.

For an eternity.

She tasted so good. She felt like heaven—her lips, her hair. But it wasn't enough. His hand swept up under her jacket, pulling the fabric of her top away with his thumb. She shuddered as he captured her breast, cupping its fullness, feeling the inviting press of her nipple against his palm. He found that tight bud, rolling it between his fingers, making her moan into his mouth.

And still it wasn't enough. Would it ever be enough? The fleeting thought was irrelevant. He wanted her, and badly. Desperation drove his actions. Anticipation fuelled his every move. He had to have her.

But, dammit, not this way!

It wasn't enough to take her. Not this time. She already thought him little more than an animal. It was time to prove to her there was more to sex than angry rutting. But first she had to want him. She had to be the one who made the first move. He drew his head back, filling his hand with her and squeezing her perfect breast one last time, committing the feel of her in his hand to memory, as he breathed in the heady scent of passion filled air.

She was drowning, battling for oxygen, battling to stay on top of a world that was reeling beneath her, battling to convince herself that she wanted him to stop. So that when he did suddenly, without warning, she felt cheated, embarrassed that it was he who had pulled out of the kiss.

'So what happens now?' She forced the words through choppy breathing and still shakier resolve. 'You throw me to the floor and take me like the caveman you are?'

'If I were going to take you, I wouldn't wait to get you to the floor. I'd take you right here, right now, hard up against this wall.'

A sizzle of sexual excitement coursed through her at the idea, until indignation snuffed it out. 'If I *were* going to take you…' he'd said.

So what was stopping him? She sure as hell hadn't been able to. She hadn't wanted his advances, hadn't gone looking for them, but that hadn't stopped her body embracing every move of his, every thrust of his tongue. If he hadn't stopped, she wasn't entirely sure she could have.

His chest heaving, his eyes guarded with new-found control, he pushed away from the wall—*away from her*—magnifying her frustration with each additional centimetre of distance he placed between them.

Damn him! Hadn't she'd known he'd do exactly this? It was this morning happening all over again. She'd known that he'd take any opportunity to arouse her and then drop her dead, hanging her out to dry.

'Thank heavens you seem to have come to your senses then,' she lied, smoothing her clothing in an attempt to appear blasé. 'I can't say I'd relish either option.'

'No? Then maybe you should tell me what option you would relish.'

'What do you mean?'

'The next time we make love—you will decide when. You will decide how.'

She hesitated, not believing what she'd heard. 'You're saying that you won't make love to me until I give you permission to?'

'No. Not until you *ask* me to.'

She threw her head back and laughed. Maybe she didn't need those contraceptive pills after all. She might be weak when it came to resisting his advances, but there was no way she'd be the one to come on to him. If he remained true to his word and left her alone, she'd already won. 'Then I hope you're a patient man, Diablo, because you're going to have a long wait.'

His eyes narrowed, a muscle twitched in his cheek.

Serves him right, she thought. He'd probably been expecting her to roll over and beg for it right here and now. 'An *awfully* long wait,' she added for good measure.

He loosened his jaw enough to utter just two tight words. 'We'll see.'

'Don't flatter yourself. Do you think you're so irresistible that I'll somehow end up begging you to make love to me?'

He said nothing for a while, just continued to regard her solemnly as they stood framed in the fading evening light, before finally he turned away, pushing open the heavy timber doors. 'I can wait.'

CHAPTER SEVEN

'WHEN are we going back to Sydney?'

On the lounger beside her, she was aware of Diablo stirring and rising up on to one elbow. At their feet the large indoor pool sparkled blue under the clear roof that let the ultraviolet rays in and turned a grey autumn day outside into an indoor summer.

'Don't tell me you're not enjoying our honeymoon?'

'No,' she said, slipping a bookmark into a novel she'd bought during their latest outing. Normally she'd never put down a book by her favourite author, but today everything was wrong, the book not holding her interest, the lounger chair feeling lumpy and uncomfortable, her bikini top straps biting into her shoulders and even the air inside the enormous climate-controlled room feeling too closed in and stuffy. 'It's very…relaxing. But how long are we staying?'

She looked at him, waiting for an answer, and immediately wished she hadn't. *And that was part of her problem.* She wanted to look away but the sight of that broad sweep of satin-smooth skin, packed with rippled muscle tone and corded tautness, wouldn't let her. How could she tear her eyes away from his tightly packed waist and the line of dark hair that led inexorably lower, when it was all she could do to breathe? In a concession to her modesty he was wearing trunks—low black trunks that accentuated more than they hid, low black trunks that had her thinking of—*had her remembering*—what lay below. Even now as she watched the fabric seemed to stir and strain, causing the blood in her own veins to slow to a crawl.

Was that why her pulse kicked up a gear? Was that why it suddenly thundered so loud in her ears—to try to force her sluggish blood from stalling in her veins?

But it wasn't just her blood. Everything, even time itself, seemed to thicken and slow.

'You're bored?'

His words drew her gaze to his face, his dark eyes reflective, brooding, his dark hair loosely tucked behind his ears. Didn't he know? Nobody could ever get bored looking at Diablo. It was like studying some nameless statue carved in marble and wondering at the man who had been so godlike as to have been chosen as the subject. Diablo, with his aristocratic features and powerful shoulders and broad chest, could have been that man, facsimile of the gods and the sculptor's choice.

She unglued her tongue from the roof of her mouth. She'd already swum more laps than she could remember today but it didn't seem nearly enough. 'I think maybe I need to do something a bit more taxing than reading.'

His mouth curved into a knowing smile. 'That could be arranged.'

'I meant—'

'I know what you meant,' he assured her, lifting himself from the lounger with fluid grace. 'There's rain predicted for later today. Why don't we go for a walk along the beach now while we can?'

He didn't have to be so accommodating, she decided, as she shrugged a sweater and track pants over her bikini. He didn't have to appear so at ease with this standoff. It had been three days since he'd told her that making love would be her call. And it had been three very long nights. He'd come to bed so late that she'd been asleep. She knew it had been late because she'd lain awake trying to read till after midnight each night, huddled in an over-sized T-shirt she'd found in the walk-in wardrobe. True to his word, he'd left her alone. True to his word, he'd not made so much as a move towards her.

Oh, she'd seen him looking plenty. She'd spied his gaze on her more than a dozen times a day, his hungry eyes unleashing a rabble of butterflies inside her, the unmistakeable signs of his body reacting to hers setting them aflutter. And, more than once, she'd felt his ravenous eyes trapping hers when they'd found her spying on him.

But so what that he caught her looking? She'd never sworn not to look. She was hardly about to do anything more than that. Besides, how would she know how he was holding up unless she did look? Given his past performances, it was more likely he'd crack under the strain than her. Though so far he was making re-sisting her seem all too easy…

But this wasn't about his powers of resistance. He'd issued her with a challenge and she was up to it. And so far she'd lasted three days. Which meant that so far she was winning the battle.

She grabbed sneakers and slammed her feet into them with a sigh of disgust.

So why did winning feel so much like hell?

Fifteen minutes later there was still no sign of Diablo. She came across the housekeeper dusting in the living room.

'Luisa, have you seen Diablo anywhere? We're supposed to be going for a walk.'

The woman looked up, a broad smile lighting up her kindly features. 'Ah, *sí*. There was a telephone call. Mr Barrentes took it in the office.'

'Oh. Maybe I'll wait here, then.' She picked up a magazine from the stack of current releases on the coffee table, prepared to wait on one of the armchairs until he emerged.

'No, no, no! Mr Barrentes works too hard. You take him for a walk. It will do him good.'

Her reluctance to interrupt Diablo while at work in his office must have shown on her face.

'You are his wife!' Luisa stressed. 'You come first, not business. Go to him—one look at you will remind him of his duty.'

Briar gave the older woman a grateful smile as she set the magazine back down. Luisa must have known this was no ordinary marriage, but still she'd made Briar feel as welcome to the role of mistress of the house as if it had been a love match.

Still, it was with a nervous tap on his open office door that she announced her presence. He was leaning back in his office chair, both feet on his desk and talking rapid fire into the phone. He looked up at the sound and beckoned her inside, pointing to his watch before holding up five fingers. She let go of a breath she'd been holding. Luisa had been right; she had no need to cower outside his office. She had a right to be here.

Diablo continued with his phone call, speaking nineteen to the dozen in a tone that made Briar glad she wasn't on the receiving end. She did her best to tune out, instead turning her attention to the pictures that lined the walls of the large office. She hadn't been here since that first night and then she'd barely crossed the threshold as Diablo had led her on a tour of the house.

A large painting held pride of place on the wall right behind her, opposite his desk, a painting of a dark-haired woman. Instantly she was struck by the resemblance. The same dark eyes, the same autocratic features, the same strength of character shining out from the dark depths of her eyes—it had to be his mother Camilla. Diablo's good looks were clearly no accident of nature.

She pulled her eyes away from the portrait while the one-sided conversation continued behind her. A collection of at least a dozen black and white photographs had been arranged over a bank of filing cabinets. At first she took them to be old school photographs from Diablo's youth, but as she drew nearer she realised they couldn't be. The crowd of smiling children were arranged in neat rows, and all dressed in the same shorts and shirts with what looked like their teachers standing either end. But they were all Hispanic or South American Indian-looking or a blend of both, the building behind looking like no school she'd ever seen in Australia— and with a name like none she'd ever seen—*La Escuela de Barrentes*.

She blinked and turned to him, to find him watching her even as his short words signalled the end of the call. With a brief, 'See to it,' he replaced the receiver.

'So, you are ready for our walk?' he said, rounding the desk towards her. 'I am sorry to have kept you waiting so long.'

'That's okay,' she answered, refusing to be shepherded from the room. 'Tell me about these pictures. Who are these children?'

He shrugged as if they were of no consequence. 'It is a school in Chile. They take in orphans and children from the surrounding regions and provide them with an education and basic needs.'

'But it has your name on it—La Escuela de Barrentes. Doesn't that mean the Barrentes School?'

'Your Spanish is surprisingly excellent.'

'You *own* a school?'

He shook his head. 'I merely sponsor it.'

Was he kidding? There had to be at least two hundred children lined up in front of that building. 'You're merely a sponsor and yet they named the school after you? That's some sponsorship. However did you get involved in that?'

He lifted a hand to the corner of the nearest photograph, straightening it slightly. 'My mother was lucky,' he answered obliquely. 'She managed to get away from Chile and start a new life. But for those left behind there was no easy escape from those times. Things are changing now but there remains continuing pockets of poverty and lack of facilities. And, had my mother not got away, I could so easily have been one of those children...'

His words trailed off.

'You wanted to give those children a chance at life, just as you had been given.'

He wrapped an arm around her shoulders as they stood there together looking at the smiling faces in the photographs. 'Children represent the future. They are important, more important than anything in the world. Don't you agree? Why do you think I am so keen to start my own family?'

Her mouth went dry. *The future.* He cared about children because he cared about the future?

'You told me you wanted children to ensure you wouldn't be thrown out of Sydney society if our marriage went belly up.'

'And you would have believed me if I'd told you anything different? I think not.'

She looked up at him in surprise. He sure had her pegged. Which was ironic considering all along she'd thought she had him neatly pigeon-holed. *Predatory, cold-hearted businessman who cared for nothing and no one except for himself and his fortune.* But he did care for others—these pictures proved it.

What else might she be wrong about?

She shook her wayward thoughts away as she returned her gaze to the photographs, but she couldn't escape the cloud of guilt that crept over her. Diablo wanted a family, maybe not borne of love, but a family and a future nonetheless. And here she was popping contraceptive pills to ensure he was denied that very chance.

Damn him! She didn't want to feel guilty! She shouldn't have to. She'd never really been consulted about the terms of this marriage. He'd never shared either his love of children or his dreams about the future with her. He'd just assumed she'd fall in with his plans and produce his progeny on demand.

And she couldn't do that or she'd never get away! And wasn't getting away what she wanted?

Confusion swirled inside her mind. Of course she did. She wanted this marriage over as soon as possible. That was her goal—a goal she had to keep fixed in her sights.

'Come,' he said, squeezing her shoulders before dropping his arm to take her hand. 'We should go before the weather deteriorates any more.'

The wind was already up outdoors, toying playfully with the ends of their hair one minute, coming in gusts that threatened to knock them over the next. He led the way down the hill path to the shore under a grey, forbidding sky, the air heavy with the promise of rain and the tiny spray of long ago crashed surf tossed on the wind. It was wild and taxing and invigorating all at the same time.

She jumped down the final two feet to the pebble-strewn beach and stood there, feeling the air refresh her soul. Coming to the beach had been a great idea. It had meant Diablo had had to put on some clothes for a start, not that he didn't know how to best fill out low-slung cut-offs and a black sweater. But at least for a while her tension had dissipated and she could stop thinking about sex and how best to avoid it.

He turned, looking for her, his eyes concerned. 'Too cold?' he yelled over the sound of the surf and the blustering wind.

She shook her head, stray tendrils whipping around her face and unable to keep the laughter from her voice. 'No. I love it.'

His features relaxed and he smiled back. 'Come on, then.'

They walked, barely talking, for what seemed like miles, following the rugged shoreline from the promontory heading towards the tiny bay around which the tiny township nestled, occasionally stopping to pick up a shell along the shore. And somewhere along the way he'd offered her his hand as she'd clambered over a rocky outcrop and somehow it had stayed there, nestled warmly within his own.

How strange, she thought, that she could be walking companionably with Diablo, the man who waited patiently while she discovered each new shell on the sand—the same man she hated most in the world. She slid a glance up at him. But did she? The last three days he'd been the perfect host—polite, thoughtful, considerate. They'd read together, discussed current events, even taken in a movie in a nearby town. And she certainly hadn't picked Diablo for someone who actively cared about the rights and needs of children.

And now they were walking hand in hand. No, just lately it wasn't hatred she felt for him at all—more like a... *fascination*. Because everything about Diablo was fascinating, from the way he moved with stealthy precision, to the way his eyes flamed when they turned on her, and the way they set spot fires burning under her skin.

And he was her first ever lover—leagues better than her few fumbling boyfriends had ever managed to be—why wouldn't she be fascinated by him? No matter how her life evolved after this, he would always remain that. It was no doubt natural she would be intrigued. Especially when he'd made it clear that he intended to make love to her again.

So how long would he wait? A man like Diablo wouldn't be used to waiting, and certainly not for a woman—a woman he believed he had every right to.

How long could he keep that civilised veneer holding up, before it cracked apart under the strain of waiting for her? She shivered. He'd overwhelmed her with his passion on their wedding night. All that power, all that potent virility, and all of it unleashed on her—*inside her*. Would it always be that way between them if she let him?

Between her thighs, her muscles clamped down at the memory of how he'd filled her, how she'd been stretched and had felt so out of control when he'd moved inside her. Which was crazy. A year, a month, a week ago she had hardly been aware of those muscles. Now they seemed determined to make their presence felt, pulsing with a strange ache that lingered even though the initial tenderness had long gone.

Why couldn't she just forget? It should have been easy to resist him, to carry out her promise of making him wait a long, long time before she succumbed. So why did she seem to spend every waking moment thinking about him—thinking about how it would feel to make love with him again—*wanting to make love with him again...*

'Briar?'

The tug on her hand pulled her from her thoughts.

'Are you okay?'

She blinked and came to, her vision filled with dark eyes that one could fall into and never be found. She shivered again and wrapped her arms around herself. 'Sorry, just deep in thought,' she admitted, looking around and taking in her surroundings, praying that he wouldn't ask her exactly what she'd been thinking about.

They'd reached the perfect horseshoe bay that fringed one boundary of the town in a sandy beach that looked today like a white lace edging. Here it was more protected from the wind, the waves still foaming their way up the shore but tamed into a more regular rhythm. It was a week day and only a handful of people dotted the beach.

'There's a café nearby if you'd like coffee.'

The wildness of their walk around the blustery point had been energizing but the relative serenity of this tiny bay was something else, especially now the sun had managed to peep out from behind the clouds. It wouldn't last. Already dark clouds loomed threateningly, a promise of the rains to come. 'I'd like to sit and watch the sea for a while, if that's okay with you, while the sun's still out. Coffee can wait,' she suggested.

He looked out to sea, his hands in his pockets, a frown

tugging at his brow, and for a moment she thought he was going to insist they move on to the café now. But then he shrugged and seemed to relent.

Diablo sat down beside her on a small rise overlooking the narrow strip of beach, leaning back and propped up on his elbows while Briar sat with her chin on her hands, her elbows propped up on her knees and her collection of shells between her feet. If she looked a distance down the coastline towards the large promontory from where they'd come she could still see the occasional burst of spray rising high as the waves beyond the bay pounded at the rock-lined shore, while here the sun felt warm and welcoming on her face.

'It's such a beautiful beach here, so sheltered and peaceful.'

'Deceptively peaceful. There's a strong rip, especially this time of year.'

His blunt words confirmed the signs she'd seen warning swimmers of the treacherous undertow. 'You wouldn't pick it,' she said, feeling lulled by the rhythm of the incoming waves. 'It's so much calmer here compared to on the point. It's hard to believe it's the same day.'

'My mother used to say it's like being in the eye of the storm. She used to walk down here and sit and read for hours.'

She swung her head around, He was talking about his mother and this time she hadn't invited him to.

'She must have loved living here,' Briar said. 'It's so beautiful. Though it must be wild to be up there where the house is when there's a storm. It must feel like being at the very end of the earth.'

His eyes fixed hers in a stare so deep and empty it seemed fathomless. And when his voice came it seemed that too came from the depths of beyond. 'My mother loved the wild weather the best. She used to say that sometimes she could hear my father talking to her on the wind. It made her feel closer to him.'

In spite of the gentle heat from the sun, Briar shivered. She could almost feel Camilla's pain reach out and touch her, the pain of a lonely woman with the hungry wind for company, carrying the cherished voices of the dead.

'That was a portrait of your mother in the study, wasn't it?'

His eyes narrowed as if he was wondering how she knew.

She smiled and hunched her shoulders up. 'The resemblance is unmistakeable. She was a beautiful woman.' She hesitated for a moment before going on. Just because he'd finally admitted he'd had a mother didn't mean he was ready to tell her everything. 'What happened to her?'

He sat up suddenly, blowing out his breath in a rush. 'A stupid accident. Something that never should have happened.'

The heavy silence following his words made it clear he wasn't about to fill her in on the details.

'I'm so sorry,' she simply said. 'My brother died in a car accident two years ago. A truck lost control, crossed the highway and ploughed into the oncoming cars. It was midnight when the police came to tell us the news.' She shivered. 'He was only twenty-six…'

She felt a hand surround hers. 'You miss him still?'

She nodded. 'It's been hardest on my parents, of course…'

She'd been going to add, *especially with the business falling apart*, but she couldn't. Besides, her parents had money now. At least that was one concern they didn't have to deal with any more.

And, no matter what Nat's death had cost her, just as devastating must have been Diablo's loss of his mother. She'd been his only family. She couldn't begin to imagine what that would do to a person.

'Your mother must have missed your father terribly. She never remarried?'

He shook his head as he looked out to the horizon. 'My father was a hero. Nobody else ever came close. Nobody else ever could.'

'They must have loved each other so very much,' she mused, 'to have given up so much and risked everything to be together.'

He swung his body around to face her, surprising her with the intensity of bitterness contained in his eyes. 'But all for what? What was the point of loving like that? What good did it do them?' He picked up a pebble lying half buried in the sand and launched it with a flick of his wrist, spinning it low over the beach. She watched it skip and roll across the sand, only half aware of the seagulls in its path that squawked and rose in a cloud, while his words jarred into focus the conversation they'd had that very first night together.

'I can see what you've got against fairy tales.'

'What are you talking about?' He sounded impatient, irritable, as if he was wishing he'd never agreed to stop and talk.

'You told me you don't put much stock in happy endings. Obviously your parents missed out on their happy ever after, so you prefer to think it doesn't exist at all.'

'Do me a favour. Don't try to psychoanalyse me.'

'Who needs to psychoanalyse when it's written all over you? You feel bitter about what your parents missed out on when their time together was cut so short.'

'And what if I am?'

'Then you must know that for every couple that meets with tragedy, there are those who are happily married, who live and love and who grow old together. Even my own parents have been married for something like thirty years. What about them? Don't their happy ever afters count?'

'All I know is that there was no fairy tale ending for my mother, and if she didn't deserve it, I don't know anyone who does.'

What could she say to that? But at least things were starting to make some kind of bizarre sense, like his high-handed attitude and his lack of consultation with her about their marriage, the honeymoon and all that went with it. All along he hadn't wanted her to be involved—to *get* involved. All along she'd been more of a possession than a partner. Once it would have made her angry—who was she trying to kid?—it *had* made her angry— but now, instead of anger, she felt a kind of aching sadness for him, that his parents' experience had robbed him of a belief in the worth of love and devotion.

It was sad. What Diablo really needed was a woman who would show him how it was possible to love and be loved. He needed a woman who could change his mind about happy endings only ever happening in fairy tales. He needed a woman who could prove it could be so.

Which was ironic really. Because instead he'd been lumbered with Briar, plotting to bail out of this sham of a marriage the first chance she got. That was really going to change his attitude about happy endings—*not*.

But then, what Diablo thought was hardly her lookout anyway. It wasn't her job to change his mind about love and marriage. He'd set up this crazy arrangement. Why should she feel guilty when it all turned to dust?

'Now I understand why you were content to settle for a marriage of convenience—not simply because I provided the right bloodlines, but because you figured there was nothing to lose if it didn't last.'

'There's no reason our marriage can't last. But you're right; you can't lose what you haven't got. My parents loved deeply and lost everything. What's the point?'

She resisted the urge to tell him there was *every* reason why their marriage wouldn't last. 'You're the point!' she said instead. 'Don't you see? They didn't lose everything. Your mother got you! Don't you think that meant something extra special to your mother—to have something of your father to live on, even after she'd lost him?'

'Sure. It meant she had to slog her guts out by herself, working around the clock to provide for me.'

'And you think she did that because you were a liability or because she loved you so much?'

He grunted, showing his displeasure with the question and she sighed. What did it matter what he thought? It wasn't her job to change his view of life, the universe and everything. Instead she watched the seagulls wheeling in circles overhead and thought about the kind of woman his mother must have been; she sounded as if she'd been there for her son twenty-four hours a day. At least that was one thing he couldn't disagree with her about.

He pushed himself up to standing, brushing off the sand from his trousers. 'I'll go and get that coffee.'

She'd made him angry again, but then, what else was new? If he wasn't teasing her, he was angry with something she'd said or done. Still, she bristled as she watched him stride purposefully away across the sand to the grass-lined main street and beyond to the small strip of shops and cafés that lined the esplanade. A table of women were sitting outside and as one their heads turned as he strode past and entered, intent on animated conversation and peering conspiratorially through the front window once he'd disappeared. She shook her head. There was no doubt who they'd be talking about. If they only knew what a hard case he was, maybe they'd know to leave well enough alone. He wasn't worth it. She turned her attention away from the admiring women and wrapped her arms around her knees.

At least now she understood his attraction to an arranged marriage. It was a no risk option. Love was never an issue with Briar—*would never be an issue*—which suited her just fine. *Just fine*, she insisted to herself as once again she contemplated the endless roll of waves lapping at the water's edge.

A few minutes later she was down there, unable to resist the temptation of dipping her toes into the water, her shells jangling in her pockets. The undertow might be dangerous, but the shallows would be safe enough. She could at least get her feet wet. She shrugged off her shoes and rolled up her track pants before strolling along the water's edge, her bare feet splashing in the wash, laughing with the whoosh as the water rushed up around her ankles on the way up the beach and the powerful suction that even in the shallows ripped the sand out from under the soles of her feet when it receded. She stooped down when the vanishing sand revealed another shell under her foot. She picked it up, washed off the sand in the shallows and looked at it, admiring its perfect shape and pastel colours. She screwed her feet into the sands again to search for more.

'What the hell do you think you're doing?'

She looked around in surprise to see Diablo striding across the sand, the look on his face as dark as the storm clouds gathering above.

'What does it look like?' she asked ingenuously. 'I'm swimming to New Zealand.'

He didn't laugh. 'I told you that water was dangerous.'

'Relax,' she soothed, wondering how long it would take him to snap out of this mood as she stepped up the sand towards him. 'The last I heard, paddling wasn't considered an extreme sport.'

She looked at his empty hands. 'Where's the coffee?'

'They're bringing it.'

Of course they were. Behind him she could see a waiter setting up a table for two on the grassy strip overlooking the beach. As she watched, a gingham check tablecloth and a tiny white vase complete with fresh flowers, was added. A waitress followed bearing a tray. Why, when he had mentioned getting coffee, had she ever imagined that he would return bearing two Styrofoam cups?

'You certainly don't do things by halves, do you?' she said as he led her over to the setting.

'And you would have preferred to drink your coffee out of some kind of disposable cup?'

'No,' she agreed as he seated her; he had a point there. She placed her treasure from the sea on the table and lifted her cup up in mock toast. 'Here's to practising safe paddling.'

He had the decency to realise he'd overreacted. He took a deep breath, looking up to the sky before returning his gaze to her, the barest glimmer of a smile turning up his lips. 'Agreed,' he said, touching cups.

'What are you planning on doing with those?' he asked, indicating the shells.

'I don't know,' she answered honestly. 'They're just so pretty; I've never been able to resist shells.'

They drank their coffee watching the storm clouds rolling ominously towards the shore, until Diablo said they should be getting back. They set off along the shore, strolling back along the way they'd come, Diablo staying just above the waterline with her shells jostling noisily in his pocket, Briar splashing her way through the foam. His eyes crinkled, the corners of his mouth turning up, as she skipped through the shallows when the waves broke, her sneakers now tied and still swinging from around her neck. 'You look like a little girl who's never been to the beach before.'

'I feel like it,' she admitted through her smile, enjoying the play of water and sand through her toes. 'I thought it would be colder down at the beach but it's just wonderful.' She squealed as a rogue wave sent a rush of water licking up the shore, intent on catching them both this time.

'Watch out!' she cried, grabbing his arm and urging him up the beach but already too late to save his hand stitched boat shoes from a drenching.

Clear of the water, he stopped to survey the damage. 'You could have warned me,' he accused.

'I did,' she said in between laughter, still holding on to his arm. 'I was just a bit late.'

He lifted his eyes to her face, joining in the laughter until something abruptly shifted between them. His eyes changed in an instant from laughter to something infinitely more dangerous and all of a sudden she was all too conscious of the muscular power of his arm under her hands, of her breasts all but brushing against him, craving contact where there was none, anticipating contact... Heat came off him in waves—sensual, wraparound heat that drew her like a magnet closer to the source, squeezing out what little air remained between them.

His eyes were on her eyes, his gaze darting between them as if reading her, searching for a reason why he couldn't—why he shouldn't—and then they narrowed and dropped to her lips as a hand gathered her in from behind, stroking her neck, its gentle pressure drawing her ever closer, sparking and shorting her circuits. And she knew in an instant what his eyes had been telling her.

He was going to kiss her.

His breathing was fast and shallow. They shared the same air, his lips parted, his mouth already angling over hers.

He was going to kiss her.

Time stood still. The whoosh of the incoming tide, the cry of the seagulls, even the distant movement of traffic in the town all seemed to blur into a single note that sounded out one inevitable truth.

He was going to kiss her.

And she was going to let him.

What harm could come of it? she reasoned with her few remaining functioning brain cells. They were standing on a beach. It could lead nowhere. It was just a kiss, after all.

And then his lips touched hers and her eyelids fell shut on a sigh. How many times had they kissed? A handful, a dozen, two dozen? Surely no more. And yet, as his lips gentled hers, caressing, coaxing, she had the irrational sense of coming home.

Without breaking contact with her mouth, he shrugged off the shoes from around her neck and gathered her in closer, surrounding her with his arms, pulling her bodily against him. From her mouth to her toes, every part of her touched some part of him, she felt every part of her buzzing with contact with him, from the tender sweet passion of his mouth and lips and tongue to the sinewy muscled tone of his calves and the rock-solid core of him that pressed hard against her belly.

Just a kiss? Who had she been trying to kid?

It hadn't been just a kiss. And, just as the sounds had merged around them, the world itself seemed to dissolve and reform. There were just the two of them here, in this moment. His hand edged around her ribcage, his thumb stroking the soft side swell of her breast, sending her senses reeling. Like a drug, she wanted more. She craved more, so that when he cupped her breast fully, his fingertips brushing the electric nub of her nipple, it gave her a momentary high that left her with a desperate thirst for more.

But then it was over. She opened her eyes, confused, feeling the cold rush of his withdrawal where before there had been such delicious heat.

'I'm sorry,' he said, his breath raspy, his forehead touching her own, his hands holding hers out to her sides. 'We should get back.'

She trembled, her mouth trying to find the sounds that would make coherent words that said something other than *why*? while tears of anger and frustration stung her eyes—insane and unnecessary. Because she knew very well why—because he'd told her she'd be the one who would choose the next time they made love. She'd be the one to make the next move.

And while at the time she'd relished the power he'd given her, the power to control his sexuality, right now some primal part of her screamed out that it didn't want it at all. Instead it yearned to be swept away by him, to have both the decision and the responsibility taken away from her.

Why was it so easy for him to stop when it was such hell for her?

A booming sound split the heavens, causing the ground and

even the air around them to shake, as icy-cold needles collided like pinpricks on her heated skin.

He cursed into the sky, taking her by the hand even as the thunderous noise reverberated in her eardrums. 'We have to get back. Come on.'

If it was a race against the rain, the rain won—no question. Before long they were both drenched to the skin, as they jogged along the shore, scrambling over rocks until finally they came to the hill path that led to the house. The wind was higher here and it whipped around them, further chilling her icy skin, the loose tendrils of her hair plastered like ice-cold wire around her face, her sweater and track pants heavy with water. How could it get so cold so quickly? She felt icy to the core.

They made it to the top, soaking and panting, and the clouds sent out a stinging burst of hail to welcome them. They squelched across the lawn and arrived sopping wet on the covered terrace.

She stopped to wrench off her heavy shoes but she was shaking too hard and lost balance.

'*Dios,*' he said, grabbing her before she fell. 'But you are frozen. Forget the shoes. You need to get warm, now.'

Diablo swung her into his arms and carried her through to their bedroom and into the spacious *en suite* bathroom, oblivious to the trail of water sloughing off behind him. 'Bath or shower?' he asked gruffly, setting her down in the middle of the room and keeping an arm around her as if she were suddenly about to keel over.

'Sh…shower,' she managed, even though she wasn't sure she'd last the distance standing up. But neither did she want to wait for the bath to fill. Diablo leaned into the extra large alcove, turning on the taps, running the water until the temperature was perfect.

Then he prised her hands from across her arms and lifted her sodden sweater, pulling it from her shoulders. He raised a foot and relieved her of one sneaker and then the other while she propped her arms, still shaking, against his back and then he eased her track pants down her goosebumped legs.

She stood there, still trembling, in just her bikini, her skin so pale, so icy-cold.

'There,' he growled, dropping his hold on her and already halfway to the door, intent on getting out of there before he did something crazy, 'I'll leave you to it.'

'Thank you.'

Her voice sounded fragile enough to snap, the tight thread running through it reeling him back. He turned. She hadn't budged from where he'd left her, her hair plastered in tendrils over her eyes, her arms crossed over the twin triangles of her bikini top. Clouds of steam billowed from the shower, enveloping her, rendering her almost ethereal, a visitor from another world. Even dripping wet, he couldn't recall having ever seen anyone more beautiful. And, for some bizarre reason, it physically ached to contemplate walking out of here and leaving her.

She was watching him with her large eyes, not moving, clearly waiting for him to go. And, *dios*, he had to get out of there! Before he did something stupid like pulling her into his arms and kissing her senseless. Rendering himself senseless. Just like he had on the shore. *So much for making a deal to wait for her.*

Because she didn't want him—not enough. She was happy to let him take the lead but she'd made clear over the last three days that she would be damned if she'd be the one to make the first move. And he damned himself for the ultimatum he'd given her. Every time he'd caught her eyes on him, all it had done was make him so hard with expectation that he hurt. But she'd pulled back from any opportunity—and there had been plenty—for them to make love.

And the hardest thing of all was to avoid her in the evenings, to wait until he was sure she would be asleep, before he was game to go to bed. It was bad enough trying to rest with her sleeping figure so close, knowing she wouldn't welcome his advances. How could he dare risk her rejection while she was still awake? While he still burned for her?

He dragged in one unsteady breath and took another step towards the door. 'You'd better get in that shower. You need warming up.'

'You need a shower, too. You're as cold as I am.'

'I can wait until you're finished. I'll be right outside if you need me.'

'No!' she protested as he had one hand on the door, her eyes even wider. 'I need you here—to hold me up.'

A gravelly sound issued uninvited from his throat—a growl—as, despite its frigid encasing, his groin kicked into life. 'If I stay here, don't expect me to stop at merely holding you up.'

She lifted her chin. 'I was hoping you might say that.'

Was he hearing her right? Her eyes were wide and glossy, her bottom lip trembling, and he wanted to wrap her up in his arms and warm her, wanted to hold her against him and hear her heartbeat meld with his, feel her body meld with his.

And he wanted those things so badly!

He took a step closer. 'Are you sure?'

'It's my choice, just like you said. I decide when. I decide how.'

She reached behind her back and he saw the strap of her bikini top fly free. Then she peeled away the fabric covering her breasts and pulled it over her head while she held out her other arm to him.

'And that time is now.'

CHAPTER EIGHT

HE swept her into his arms in a heartbeat, capturing her in a tangle of limbs. Immediately he was struck by just how cold she was, like a marble statue, her lips icy, her skin chilled to the touch, and he wanted to breathe life into her, to lend her some of the heat building so rapidly to furnace levels below. Her mouth opened up beneath his on a sigh and she drank in his warmth willingly.

She tasted of salt like the sea spray, she tasted fresh like the teeming icy rain, she tasted of the energy unleashed between the earth and the sky in the height of the storm.

He whirled with her through the steam, spinning her into the shower recess, kicking off no more than his shoes on the way. His clothes were already drenched; it didn't matter where they came off.

He directed her under the stream of warm water, holding her there while she trembled and recovered, letting the warm torrent cascade over her, eradicating the cold chills from her flesh. And before long her trembling subsided and she stretched, reaching up her arms, arching her back under the flow, raising her face into the stream and lifting her breasts up high before him.

He groaned and gave thanks as he contemplated their creamy perfection in the mist. He was only human after all, he would never have lasted another day waiting for her and here she was, offering herself up to him. And somehow thanks didn't seem anywhere near enough.

His fingers trailed down her throat, exploring the sculpted beauty of her shoulders and chest before capturing each breast and feeling their sensual weight. He dipped his mouth to one perfect bud and supped of both her tender flesh and the water that cascaded over her, tasting the very essence of her with it.

She shuddered as he suckled, but this time he knew it wasn't with the cold. This time it was heat, pure carnal heat that set her flesh trembling in his mouth. Her hands grasped for his head, his shoulders as she groaned. But he was already moving, sliding his hands down the concave curves of her waist and over the flare of her hips, his tongue dancing around her navel. His fingers hooked into the sides of her bikini pants, peeling them down, revealing that triangular clutch of curls guarding her most feminine treasures. She held on to his shoulders as he eased her feet out of the tiny garment, running his hands up the long delicious length of her legs while he kissed her belly and pressed her to his mouth.

'You're so beautiful,' he murmured against her flesh, 'so perfect.'

Her hands cradled his head, her fingernails raking through his hair, tangling themselves in its length. He leaned back, watching his hands scoop around her legs and rise up in between.

'Diablo,' she cried out, her fingers stilled and clutching handfuls of hair, as if sensing what he had in mind.

'Are you still cold?' he asked as his fingers gently parted her, exposing her to him.

He was rewarded by her sudden gasp, which turned into a breathy, 'ohmigod' as he pressed his mouth to her, circling that tight pink bud with his tongue.

And the water streamed down as he knelt before her, worshipping her body with his tongue, discovering another taste, another texture to her, another dimension to the complex woman who was his wife.

His woman.

He spread her legs wider with his hands and cupped her sex, holding her to him as she writhed in his mouth, her breathing coming fast and furious. She was hot and ready and so damned tempting and there was no way he could resist temptation now. He slipped one, and then two fingers into her slick, tight space, immediately rewarded by the feeling of her muscles contracting around him.

'Please,' she panted, her voice a desperate cry for release coming to him through the steam and the water. 'I need you.'

She wasn't the only one in need of release. Another part of him ached to occupy that same place and satisfy its own desperate need. He pulled off his sweater and flung it into the corner, where it landed with a wet slap. She wrapped her arms around his neck while he stood and kissed her open-mouthed, unbuttoning his cargo pants, letting the weight of the water drag them down his legs, and suddenly her hand was there, cupping his throbbing length through the fabric of his underwear. Breath hissed through his teeth as she eased the band over, liberating him. *Freedom.* But right now it wasn't freedom he craved. Only in confinement would come release and right now it was the sweet imprisonment of her body he needed more than anything in the world.

'You're playing with fire,' he warned her, removing her hand and placing it back around his neck.

He lifted her high, wrapping her legs around his waist while their lips and tongues danced together. And then he let her down slowly, finding that sweet spot, testing it, letting her absorb his length as he gradually lowered her all the way down.

It was all she needed. In a charge as potent as electricity, muscles clenched and spasmed around him, her head thrown back, legs kicking as she exploded in his arms.

And something inside him burst into life. He wanted to howl

at the moon; he wanted to yell his elation from the mountains of the world. Instead he buried his face in her neck and squeezed her tighter. She was his woman. Unmistakably his.

And he would never let her go.

Her tremors were too much for him and, like a siren's call to a sailor at sea, her climax drew him inexorably closer to his own end. Now that she was quietening, he braced her against the wall, moving inside her tight depths, her unbelievably sweet, tight depths. She matched his movements, angling herself to receive each thrust, encouraging him with her small sighs of pleasure until, with a cry of triumph, he too became shipwrecked on the shore.

Oh, wow! Her senses were reeling, her lungs battling to get her breathing under control and her mind was blank except for that one thought. Oh, wow!

He pressed against her, still inside her, as he let her legs slowly slip to the floor. Amazingly enough, her knees didn't buckle under her. Then he lifted his head and smiled. 'You're beautiful,' he said, kissing her so tenderly that tears formed in her eyes. And then he smiled at her as if she were the most special being in the entire world.

Tenderness. She had never expected it from Diablo. Every time it took her by surprise. And every time it further weakened her resolve.

He wasn't supposed to be gentle.

He wasn't supposed to have a heart.

And she wasn't supposed to want to make love to him.

So much for supposition.

He drew back, pumping some shower gel into his hands.

'What are you doing?' she asked shakily. She'd imagined that now they'd had sex, they would dry off and continue their day.

'What are you supposed to do in a shower?' he asked her. 'I'm washing you.'

Her ideas on what showers were for had just expanded in new and wonderful directions, and washing seemed to be the least interesting of any of them, until he touched her with hands made slippery with the soap, running sensuously up and down her skin with devastating effect. He soaped her body, he glided his hands over her almost as if he were sculpting her, he washed and rinsed her hair and, just as he was about to turn off the taps, she found her voice.

'Oh, no,' she said, before squeezing gel into her own hands. 'I'm not finished yet.'

His pupils dilated and she smiled up at him with more nerve than she felt. 'My call,' she reminded him.

Emboldened by their lovemaking, she set about her task, sliding her hands down each arm and up again, seeking out each indentation, each swell of muscle, each nub of bone, reading him like a blind person read Braille. His shoulders, his chest, his legs—her hands traced the toned perfection of his body; she drank it all in. It was another exercise in discovery, a fascinating journey that taught her more about the male form than she would ever have learned from a thousand books. A fascinating journey that ended in a fascinating place. She skimmed her hands down his sides once more, kissing a trail down the centre of his abdomen and lowered herself to kneel before him.

He groaned as she took him in her hands. He hissed through his teeth when she circled the tip of his erection with her tongue. His knees all but buckled when she took his satin-finished flesh into her mouth and cupped his tight, tight sac in her hand. She heard him utter her name and a feeling like no other coursed through her. She was here with Diablo Barrentes and yet she felt alive, in control and very, very aroused. His hands tangled in her hair, his hips undulating rhythmically with her, unable to remain still as she paid homage to him. She tasted the salt of his juices and he grasped her head, pulling himself away.

'Not like this,' he whispered hoarsely, as he lifted her under her arms and pinned her against the tiled wall, 'when I would rather join with my woman like this…'

My woman.

She shuddered in his arms, opening herself up to him. So how was it that those very words put a sensual thrill down her spine like no other when she'd objected to his use of that expression before?

His woman. She was his woman. And insanely, irrationally, suddenly ecstatic to be so. Because today she'd discovered the flip side of being his woman.

Today she'd discovered that being his woman made him her man.

Her man pushed into her then, forcing the breath from her lungs, and once again she was reminded of his power and his sheer masculinity, delighting in it, embracing it, and then she thought of nothing at all as he withdrew before surging back into her. She did the only thing she could. She clung to him, going with him, feeling the rhythm feeding into her soul and building into something real, something concrete, something magnificent, before he tipped them both over the edge and it was lights showering down on her, splinters of light that twinkled like fireflies dancing around her.

Afterwards he wrapped her, spent and weak, in an enormous bath sheet and carried her to their bed, peeling back the covers and laying her down almost reverentially amidst the pillows and cushions.

Never had she felt more cherished.

Never had she felt more confused.

'How are you feeling?'

Extraordinary. Exquisite. Loved.

Loved?

She stared up at him blankly. Oh, no way! To imagine that would be to let what had happened in the shower go right to her head. *Shell-shocked.* Now there was a better word for what she was feeling. She was simply shell-shocked. At least that much made sense. At least that would explain this strange feeling inside her.

'You're not still cold?'

Heavens, no. Far from it. Luxuriantly warm, infinitely cosseted maybe, but *definitely* not cold. She shook her head, trying to get hold of a world that looked the same as every other day but now felt completely different. 'Shouldn't we be getting ready for dinner?'

'Luisa sent in a tray while we were showering.' He wheeled a trolley over and lifted a plate. 'There's soup and sandwiches. Are you hungry?'

'Not really,' she admitted, knowing that whatever this strange new sensation inside her was, it wasn't hunger driving it.

He climbed into bed alongside her and picked up her hand, kissing the back of it. 'You have to eat,' he said, his eyes glinting up at her suggestively. 'You need to keep up your strength.'

She started to laugh, at first nervously, but he tugged gently on the towel surrounding her, unwinding it from her body, drawing it slowly away, unwrapping her like some precious find, and her laughter changed course—deeper, more sensual and full of meaning. Then, once she was totally uncovered, she stopped laughing and he smiled at her and touched her breast, caressing it, coaxing her nipple into hardness between his thumb and forefinger before dipping his mouth and circling her nipple with his tongue while he glided his hand down her ribcage to her abdomen.

'And you need strength not just for you.' He held his hand still over the surface of her flat belly. 'Is it possible that already my child grows deep within you?'

Oh, God! She turned her head away, a stab of guilt so deep slashing into her that she couldn't face him. Hell, no, it wasn't possible at all that she was already pregnant, not with her popping pills to ensure the exact opposite. But she was hardly about to admit that.

Damn him! Why did he have to be so gentle? Why did he have to be so tender? Why did he have to make it so darned difficult for her? It was the kind of knowledge that deserved to be flung in his arrogant face, not to feel guilty about, and after the way they'd just made love, she was in no rush to spoil the mood.

'It—it doesn't always happen right away,' she faltered, frustrated, still unable to bring her eyes around to meet his. 'Sometimes it takes time—months, even longer. You can't expect…'

His hand hooked under her chin, slowly bringing her around to face him.

'Don't worry,' he soothed, clearly mistaking her hedging for a fear that she wouldn't conceive quickly enough for his liking. 'We have all the time in the world.'

'And if it's not that simple?'

'It's that simple,' he told her. 'You've seen how perfectly we fit together; you have nothing to worry about. And you will make a wonderful mother. Your babies will be beautiful and it is no wonder when I look at how beautiful you are.' He kissed her sweetly on each eyelid as if to reassure her. His dark eyes glinted knowingly as he made a sound like a low growl in the back of his throat. '*Dios*. I thought I was hungry for food, but it is you I hunger for. You left me starving for far too long.'

He dipped his mouth and kissed her lips, the next he directed at her throat and, as he took aim for the third time Briar knew she was down for the count.

Swamped in Diablo's white robe, Briar stood in the dimly lit *en suite* bathroom and stared at herself in the mirror, expecting to find something that would explain this change. Because there had to be something, some physical evidence why she felt so radically different.

What was happening to her?

A week ago, even just a few days ago, she'd been determined, she'd been certain of her path. She'd decided that she was going to be a spectator to this marriage for as long as it lasted and then she was going to get herself the hell out of there, her sense of self intact, her identity preserved.

But, heaven help her, she wasn't just a spectator any more. She was getting drawn in. Deeper and deeper drawn in with the one person with whom she'd sworn she'd never get involved. She was losing her resolve. Losing her determination. Losing herself in a man with flashing dark eyes and powerful arms that cradled her as if she was the most precious thing on earth.

What the hell was wrong with her? Surely she couldn't be starting to have feelings for him?

It couldn't be true. Diablo was great sex—great mind-blowing sex, as it happened—but it was nothing more than lust, a mere temptation of the flesh. And just because in a moment of weakness she'd given in to that temptation didn't mean she could be so easily swayed from her determination—did it? She searched her features in the mirror, looking for some sign, some evidence that she had changed. She delved into the reflection of her eyes, hoping to find the key.

What was happening to her? What had possessed her?

Possession.

Like a kick in the gut, that word shoved her thoughts right back to their love-making, right back to that pivotal moment when he'd called her his woman. And that moment later when she'd been blindsided by a thunderbolt—that Diablo was her man.

His woman. Her man. Even now the concept poured a warm flush of excitement through her veins that frightened her senseless. Surely just a surge of hormones or a moment of insanity. It had to be insanity.

She stared into the mirror, her eyes staring back—wild, unsure, clouded with trepidation.

Because, if it wasn't insanity, it didn't just mean she was starting to have feelings for Diablo. It meant she was in danger of falling in love with him.

In love with Diablo?

Please, no! She gripped the edge of the marble vanity unit to prevent herself from reeling. Diablo was ruthless, an arrogant take-no-prisoners businessman who put the pursuit of wealth above everything else in the world. He'd railroaded her into marriage, he'd cajoled her into his bed.

Except the ruthless businessman had turned one hundred and eighty degrees and shown her he had a softer side, a side that saw him giving thanks for the opportunities he'd been given by supporting the lives of children who otherwise wouldn't have a chance.

And today he hadn't had to cajole her into bed at all. Today she'd invited him to take her. She rolled her eyes heavenwards as with a chill of recognition she realised that was what had changed.

Diablo was no longer merely the jailer of her body for the term of this marriage. Diablo now possessed the keys to her will. He'd unlocked her defences—the defences she'd prided herself upon, the defences she'd relied upon in defying him, in proving she didn't want him.

And if he could do that, then how long would it be before he found the keys to her heart?

Her breath snagged in her throat. It couldn't happen, could it? Surely people couldn't change the way they felt about someone that quickly. Unless…? There was a name for it when people acted illogically towards their captors, sympathising with them, feeling a strange loyalty to them, maybe even falling in love. Stockholm syndrome, that was it. Maybe that was what was happening to her? Whisked away from her own world by her captor to a lonely house, forced to endure hour after hour in his company, was it any wonder that her feelings would soon get scrambled and rearranged? She was a captive bride, held prisoner by a man who wanted to make her his by breaking down her resistance piece by piece.

She gazed at her reflection in the mirror. So it *was* a form of insanity, then. She wasn't really having feelings for Diablo; it was their forced proximity playing on her feelings of entrapment. Things would feel different when they returned to Sydney. Things, and her emotions, would soon get back to normal.

With new resolve, she pulled out the drawer she'd taken for her own and found the small cosmetic bag she'd come in for in the first place. She zipped it open and pulled out the packet of pills, counting them. Five pills left for this month. Five pills. And then what?

For a while there she'd been in two minds as to what to do. Diablo's love of children had taken her by complete surprise, as had his sponsorship of an entire school in Chile. He'd had her feeling strangely sympathetic for his wish for children and suddenly guilty for working against his plans.

She couldn't make any rash decisions. But why should she feel so guilty when she'd been the one pushed and coerced into this marriage from the outset? Why should she feel guilty simply because she had no desire to perform the role of his personal incubator?

He'd never asked her if she wanted children. He'd certainly never asked her if she would mind having his. She'd been told, commanded, bossed into what he thought was submission without a shred of consultation and he'd assumed that once he'd locked her up long enough she'd fall in with his plans.

She popped the tiny bubble and swallowed the pill before stashing the rest away.

To hell with his plans.

He should have been asleep—had almost been asleep—but her sudden departure from the bed had him waiting, his blood quietly thrumming, anticipating her return so he could once again tuck her body in close to his.

Making love with her today had been better than great. He'd known she'd come to him—had only had a moment's doubt that she'd eventually capitulate—and although it had been his own private hell while she'd resisted, in all that time he'd had no idea just how sweet her surrender would be.

It had been heaven to take his time with her, to explore every curve and indentation of her body, to have her explore his. And now there would be time for so much more.

He heard the click of the light switch in the *en suite* bathroom and her quiet footfall across the floor, even though it was clear she was doing her utmost not to disturb him. He sensed the dull swish of his robe as she let it fall from her shoulders, a glimmer of moonlight now the storm had passed turning her skin to pearlescent perfection, before she eased her naked body into the bed.

And he felt her withdrawal from him like a slap in the face as she eased herself gently on to the edge of the mattress and lay down with her back to him.

He suppressed a snarl. After what they'd shared today there was no way he was letting her slide back into some kind of reluctant virgin persona once again.

'Hey,' he said, voicing his protest in the gentlest way he could under the circumstances.

The way her breath hitched short told him he'd surprised her. After a second her head rolled slightly around.

'I thought you were asleep.'

'Come here,' he growled, reaching out for her, intending to draw her close within the circle of his arms. And she came, but instead of melting against him as he'd been anticipating, he gathered an awkward bundle of tangled limbs and reluctant flesh. It seemed to take an eternity to settle her body's suddenly different components in his arms, and even then they felt uncomfortable and stiff, transmitting their discomfort to him in spades.

'What's wrong?' he asked, when for the third time she'd found reason to fidget rather than settle.

'Who said anything was wrong?'

'You're saying everything is all right?'

'I'm just tired. I need to sleep.'

'Then maybe you should try to sleep, rather than fighting with me.'

'I'm not fighting.'

'Good, because you'd be in for a disappointment.'

'You're so sure of yourself, aren't you? You think you know it all.'

I wish, he thought, wondering what the hell was going on in her head. He pulled her tighter in his arms. 'Go to sleep.'

CHAPTER NINE

'I HAVE to get back to Sydney,' Diablo told her the next morning over his *Financial Review* as she joined him for breakfast. 'Something's come up that I need to deal with personally.'

'So soon?' she responded, sitting down opposite him. 'The honeymoon's over, then?'

He arched an eyebrow at her. They'd made love first thing this morning before he'd gone to do some laps and then to his office to catch up with his emails, and he'd assumed from her energetic response to his love-making that she was over her 'tiredness' of last night. Apparently not. But given the reason for this morning's dash back to Sydney, he wasn't exactly in the mood to put up with it either. 'I thought you'd be pleased, seeing you didn't want a honeymoon in the first place.'

She shrugged and poured herself a coffee. 'And still we came. So what I think is hardly going to make a difference anyway.'

He regarded her levelly while she selected a piece of toast and spread it with blackberry jam, her eyes never once making the effort to travel anywhere near his. He carefully folded his newspaper in half and placed it down on the table, every movement calm and quiet while his blood simmered inside. Nobody, but nobody, blew so hot and cold with him like this woman did and got away with it.

Dammit, nobody else had the audacity to even try!

'I thought maybe we could come back here next weekend,' he continued, keeping his voice level despite the provocation, 'seeing you seemed to enjoy it here so much.'

'If you like,' she offered, munching on her toast solemnly before taking a sip of coffee.

'Perhaps we could walk along the beach again if the weather is fine.'

'Perhaps.'

'Or maybe this time you'd prefer to try something different?'

Obviously sick of contemplating her vanishing toast, her eyes slid beachwards. 'Whatever you decide, it's fine with me.'

'Done. I have just the thing in mind. I'm going to throw you down on this table in the middle of breakfast, rip your clothes from your body and make passionate love to you.'

She was halfway to a nod when her head swung around, her eyes opening wide. They collided with his, amber guns ablaze, colour flaming her cheeks.

Got you, he thought.

'What the hell are you trying to prove?'

'Sex on toast,' he taunted, feeling suddenly jauntier than he had any time since she'd sat down. 'Sure beats bacon and eggs. Then again, I'm still a bit peckish; maybe we needn't wait till next weekend.' He pushed himself out of his chair and paused for a moment, doing his damnedest to look predatory. 'I'm willing... What's to stop us going for it right now?'

Her chin jerked up, the slash across her cheeks brighter still. 'Maybe you might think to ask first.'

He smiled. 'You already acquiesced, I seem to recall. Whatever I decide is fine with you—or words to that effect.'

She glared at him for a moment before her own chair scraped back across the terrazzo-tiled floor and she stood, her stance showing she was ready for flight. 'What time do we have to leave? I have to pack.'

'You've hardly touched your breakfast.'

She threw her napkin down on her half-eaten toast. 'I've had enough.'

And so had he. 'What the hell's wrong with you?' he demanded, catching up with her as she turned and wheeled away, giving up all pretence of staying cool. 'Yesterday you couldn't wait to get me into that shower. Today you're acting like some prickly virgin.'

This time she did look him in the eyes and he took the full brunt of the topaz fire she turned on him. 'I apologise for my inexperience. Obviously, if sexual experience had been part of your selection criteria, you might have chosen a woman who satisfied your requirements one hell of a lot more closely.'

'I wasn't looking for experience.'

'No, you're absolutely right. You were looking for someone who wasn't in a position to say no. Lucky me,' she said, the irony dripping from her words while her eyebrows rose to accentuate her words, 'I drew the short straw.'

They made the journey back to Sydney in stony silence, Diablo's mood getting blacker with each passing kilometre.

He'd had her. For twelve hours yesterday she'd been his, body and soul. She'd mirrored his wavelength, she'd moved like an extension of him. She'd been his for the taking and he'd devoured what she'd offered like a starving man.

He'd always believed she was perfect for his needs, and on their wedding night he'd had an inkling of just how perfect. But yesterday she'd blown away all his expectations. She was better than perfect. She was a goddess and, wherever that goddess had gone, he wanted her back.

He thought back over the hours she'd almost seemed part of him. There was nothing he could think of that had made her angry. On the contrary, she'd seemed as blown away by the sheer impact of their love-making as he'd been himself. Then, without warning, she'd locked herself into the bathroom, only to return a changed woman, the goddess vanquished, replaced with a sassy-mouthed she-cat who was happier sparring than making love.

He thumped the heel of his hand against the steering wheel. The amber-eyed she-cat alongside him barely acknowledged the sound, still resolutely gazing out the windows.

The sports car negotiated its way through the building traffic with a throaty roar. He took the freeway heading for the city and, as they passed the turn-off for Mosman, finally she found her voice.

'Where are we going?'

'To my apartment.'

'But I thought you might drop me off…' Her words trailed off and he allowed himself a smile.

'You thought I might drop you off at your parents' house? But why? You're my wife now. You live with me.'

'I thought you had to work. What will I do?'

'Get acquainted with your new home.'

'I don't even know where you live.'

'Then you'll soon find out.'

She turned her head to look out the window so he couldn't read her face and take satisfaction from her disappointment. Truth was, she could have found out about where Diablo lived, plenty of times, if she'd bothered. But she'd never bothered. She'd never even broached the subject. She'd never wanted to know anything about the man or his private life, had never sought the information, even after she'd learned of their engagement, preferring to avoid thinking about her future as much as possible. Now she wished she hadn't been quite so blinkered. She might feel more prepared.

'What about all my things?' she asked, swinging her head around to look at him. 'And my car?'

'Packed, delivered and waiting for you. All efficiently taken care of while we were away.'

'You certainly didn't waste any time.'

'Wasting time is not the way I work.'

She rolled her eyes. 'I hadn't noticed,' she muttered, before turning her attention out of the window to the looming outline of Sydney CBD.

She descended back into silence, her hopes for a return to sanity and clear-thinking taking a sharp dive. She'd been crazy to imagine he'd let her out at Blaxlea before he went to work. It was hope that had blinkered her thoughts, hope that when they were back in Sydney life might take on some sort of normality once again. But how could life return to anything approximating normal when she would still be imprisoned in Diablo's world? All he was doing in moving her from El Paradiso to his own home was merely replacing one gilded prison cell with another.

She drew in a deep breath and let it out slowly. Okay, so she had to get used to new digs. At least it was in Sydney and not halfway up the coast. He'd still be working most of each day— and she'd have her car. So she might be in prison, but not necessarily in isolation. She would cope. And she'd soon rationalise those bizarre feelings she'd been having about this man she'd married.

They crossed the Sydney Harbour Bridge and took an off ramp for the city centre. A few minutes later Diablo steered the car into an underground car park at the base of a multi-storey office block.

'I thought you were going home first.'

'This is home.' He pulled the car into a secure garaged area. 'And there is your car,' he said, indicating the neat Honda coupé beside them, 'just as I told you.'

He led her to the private lift, pressed a button for the penthouse and stood silently next to her as the lift carried them the forty-plus floors to the top. The doors slid open to a plush entrance lobby, complete with marble floor and massive timber doors curving in an arc around the lobby. He unlocked the doors and regarded her for a few moments, a hint of amusement curving his lips. 'Isn't it traditional at this point that I carry you over the threshold?'

'I am impressed,' she blistered, her eyebrows raised in mock salute. 'I didn't realise cavemen had traditions—beyond clubbing women over the head and dragging them back to their cave, that is.

'And, just in case you're tempted,' she added for good measure, 'you've already done that.'

His amusement dissolved into a scowl as she swept past him into the spacious apartment and she wondered if she hadn't overplayed her hand. It was one thing to make sure she didn't fall for his charms, it was another entirely to antagonise him into something much more dangerous. And she knew exactly how dangerous he could be when provoked. So when the hell would she ever learn to bite her tongue and not provoke him? It was a line she had to be careful not to cross.

She came to a halt inside the spacious living area, pretending to take an interest in her elegant surroundings. She knew she'd been less than pleasant company since this morning. Waspish, snippy and downright rude—and that was when she hadn't been sulking in silence. As a defence against her wayward feelings it wasn't going to earn her any friends, but she wasn't looking to be friends, not with a man who treated her like his latest corporate acquisition, more interested in the return she'd pay rather than her inherent value.

But what alternative did she have? She had to do something to shore up her defences against this man, defences that had all but tumbled down as easily he'd tumbled her once more under his warm body this morning.

How quickly he'd aroused her, his hands weaving their magic on her skin, his sculpted body fitting with hers. How skilfully he'd made her cry out with release before he'd followed her with his own guttural cry of triumph. *How ashamed she'd felt that he could reduce her to a combination of irrational nerve-endings and pulsating flesh.*

Thank goodness he'd left to go swimming before he'd seen her own eyes swimming—behind the tears of frustration that he'd left her to deal with. Because how could she hate him when he made her feel so good? And how could she *not* hate him when to him she was just a body, just a wife, just a potential incubator for his children?

'The living room,' he indicated with a sweep of his arm as if he'd taken her silence for interest in her surroundings. He then gestured with three decisive strokes of his hand. 'The kitchen, dining room and that's the study through there. There's also a full bathroom downstairs in addition to a powder room. Bedrooms are upstairs.'

She battled to look interested when all that struck her was how different it was to the house they'd just left that morning. Where El Paradiso was a rambling hacienda, full of colour and different levels and a surprise around every corner, this apartment was a statement to executive neutrality. Cool blonde timbers, caramel-coloured furniture and beige rugs adorning a light marble floor. Almost every horizontal surface was polished—and practically bare.

She wandered through to the dining room, where beige up-holstered chairs sat rigid like tombstones. How appropriate, she thought, half expecting to see a dining table in the shape of a coffin. A feature wall behind the dining table proudly boasted fawn paint instead of taupe. *Some feature.*

'This looks homely,' she said, with just a touch of irony as she ran her fingertips along a white oak buffet unit, wondering if her duty statement as wife extended as far as redecorating.

'It's home,' he said flatly. 'Make yourself comfortable. I have some affairs to attend to.'

He wandered back towards the front doors and this time his words earned a reaction. 'You're leaving? Leaving me here? What do you expect me to do?'

He shrugged. 'Become familiar with the apartment. It's your home now, too.'

He picked up his keys from the side table by the front door where he'd left them. 'I shouldn't be too late.'

'And if I want to go out?'

'Where do you need to go?'

'I don't know.' She threw her arms out wide. 'Is there a clause in my contract that says I'm to be kept in solitary confinement?'

'Don't be ridiculous,' he snapped back. 'I was just asking what you had in mind.'

'Who knows?' she insisted. 'Lunch, visiting my mother, shopping?' She seized on the last word as if it was a lifesaver. 'I'm betting the fridge is as overcrowded as the rest of this apartment.'

His eyes revealed more surprise than rebellion at that comment. 'You intend to go grocery shopping?'

'What else do you plan on eating tonight?'

He sent one dark eyebrow skywards. 'You never told me you had such a keen interest in the kitchen.'

Her own eyebrow arched in response. 'You never asked.'

He wasn't about to admit it. He merely pulled out a tiny drawer in the hall table, holding out a card. 'Here's a key. That will get you into the private lift and the entrance doors. Your car has already been fitted with a remote for the garage.' He hesitated for just a moment as he looked at her. 'Maybe going out is a good idea. At least then you might be able to summon up a smile on my return.'

She sighed and looked at the floor, feeling like a child who'd been rebuked for whingeing too long, knowing that she had, and wondering just what the hell she could have done instead.

'I'm just tired,' she said. Tired of being on alert, tired of playing cat and mouse with her emotions.

'Still tired?' he asked. 'Or maybe suffering PMT? If it's the latter, then the sooner we get you pregnant the better.'

She glared at him. 'And maybe I just don't like you. Ever consider that?'

He merely scowled and looked at his watch. 'I have to go. I'll see you later.'

'Apparently,' she said.

He paused, one hand on the door, looking over his shoulder at her. 'You wouldn't go doing anything stupid, would you?'

'Define "stupid",' she responded, crossing her arms.

He made a sound like a dull roar and abandoned the door, letting it swing closed as he swept her up in his arms. '*This* is stupid,' he growled, as his lips clamped down on hers. Shock held her rigid. Until his heat melted it clean away. Dark velvet heat filled her mouth, capturing her senses, liquefying her bones. She unwound her arms and clung to him desperately, knowing that if he let go she'd fall without that solid anchor of muscle and bone to hold her up. They exchanged lips and breath and tongues, all of it the taste of longing, the texture of desire. They exchanged the thumping pulse of blood everywhere their bodies touched, their blood dancing to the beat of the most primitive of drums.

And when finally he withdrew from the kiss, his breathing ragged, his eyes wild, it was like a punch to her gut.

'*Dios*,' he said, setting her upright, letting her go. 'I must be crazy,' he said, before turning to let himself out of the apartment.

The door closed with a hushed click. Beyond its thick sound-proofing the bing of the lift doors was but a shadow of a sound. But she heard it. Just as she was sure she heard the lift doors sliding shut. And just as she was sure she heard the ragged beat of his heart echoing hers all the way to his office somewhere below.

* * *

He must be going mad. Diablo fastened a tie around his thrumming throat and waved a passing hello to his PA as he headed for his office. She nodded a greeting and mouthed 'he's waiting inside' before returning to her typing.

He must be going mad. There could be no other explanation for the fact he wanted the very woman who was driving him crazy. She was driving him mad. She was like quicksilver, first rolling one way and then the other and just when he thought he had her she would roll away again, totally unable to be either controlled or contained.

But that kiss… If he hadn't had this meeting that kiss would never have stopped there. Dammit all—why did she have to make this so difficult?

The private investigator stood as Diablo entered. 'Paul—' he nodded, shaking hands briefly, while turning his mind to the present crisis '—has it been confirmed?'

The heavy-set man nodded, his square ex-cop jaw resolute. 'I'm sorry, Diablo. But your friend is up to his old tricks again. And we've got the evidence this time, plenty of it.'

'Damn! It wasn't just a one-off, then?'

'Not according to last night's pictures.'

'Show me.'

The investigator handed over the manila envelope, waiting in silence until his employer had had time to digest the first few pictures at least.

'And there's more.'

'Tell me,' said Diablo, sliding the photographs into a folder on his desk.

'He was heard saying he wouldn't stop until he'd got it all back—with interest. Starting tonight.'

With a crunch Diablo slammed his fist into the desk.

'He has to be stopped, once and for all.'

Paul nodded. 'Agreed.'

'And tonight. This has to end.'

'I'll take care of it,' said the investigator.

'No,' said Diablo, dismissing him. 'Fill me in on the details. I'll take care of this myself.'

CHAPTER TEN

THE apartment felt as welcoming as it was colourful. Briar wandered from room to room, checking out her new home, trying to get a handle on what it told her about Diablo. But it was odd. Where Diablo was hot, passionate and driven, this penthouse seemed cold and impersonal. Beautiful but bland. And, while Diablo had a regal kind of Spanish beauty, nobody would describe him as bland.

She strolled through the master suite upstairs, unsurprised to see that neutral had been the decorator's catchword even here. She glanced into the enormous *en suite* bathroom, hoping that at least here there would be something that might tell her about the man she'd married, but even his toiletries had been hidden away beneath the wide vanity that ran the entire length of one wall. She opened one cupboard door and, with a start, came face to face with her own belongings. He hadn't been joking when he'd said all her stuff had already been moved. He'd omitted to tell her they'd been moved by the neat police.

Two doors along she found Diablo's toiletries. Not a huge collection. But then he didn't look like a man who fussed and preened over his appearance. He didn't need to. One lonely bottle of aftershave. She popped the top and took a whiff. She recognised it. Diablo had worn it at the engagement party and at the wedding. But not since then. He seemed to prefer his own particular brand of testosterone for his signature scent.

She returned to the master suite and threw open the shuttered wardrobe doors. Just as Diablo had promised, her clothes occupied half the width of the wardrobes, all hanging more neatly than she'd ever seen them.

She shivered. It was odd. All her things were here and yet she felt like an intruder, as if she didn't belong. Suddenly it was all too much. It was all too forced. She slammed shut the doors and raced down the stairs.

Thank goodness he'd agreed to give her a key. She couldn't stay here, not in this house with no soul. He had to let her make changes—lots of them—if he expected her to live here.

On the way out she checked the refrigerator. Just as she'd suspected, it boasted little more than a tub of butter, a wedge of Camembert and a handful of beers. She picked up her bag and the key Diablo had left and let herself out. She'd soon fix that.

Her mother was home. Good. Briar snapped shut her mobile phone and stashed it in her bag, before steering her car from the underground car park into the flow of traffic.

It was good to be home, back in Sydney and at the wheel of her car. A vehicle behind tooted its horn, protesting her opportunistic change of lanes and for the first time that day she let herself smile. The busy Sydney streets felt alive and full of energy after the soundproofed neutrality of the penthouse. She didn't care that it was cool with a light drizzle starting up; she pressed a button, letting her window slide down, inviting the hum of the city to surround her. She breathed deeply. She felt alive again, almost back to normal.

Almost. She was still married to Diablo.

And what had she learned of her husband today? Only that he must spend more time in his office than the penthouse, more time eating out, more time living.

The penthouse was obviously little more than his dormitory, a glorified hotel room within easy reach of his desk. Just another of his long list of possessions. *Just like her.*

As she neared the house she still considered her home, the road wound through suburbs lined with small shops, outside which were parked every model of BMW and Mercedes imaginable. Tables covered with umbrellas or protected with blinds spilled on to the pavement and the smell of good coffee, toasted foccacia and wood-fired pizza drifted out to her. Her stomach rumbled. It had been hours since breakfast—what little breakfast she'd eaten. As soon as she arrived home she'd raid the pantry. Now the staff were back, she might even be able to wangle Mavis into making her a sandwich.

The rain came harder now and she closed her window against it. Minutes later, she pulled into the long semicircular driveway and saw her mother waving to her from the garden. 'Whatever are you doing?' asked Briar, getting out of the car as her mother pulled off her gloves to give her a hug. 'You'll get drenched.'

'Just some dead-heading and neatening up. I've got the bridge club here tomorrow and I want everything looking nice for them.' She looked at her daughter for a moment. 'Oh Briar, it's so lovely to see you. Come inside.'

'It's great to see you too,' Briar said, smiling as she waited for her mother to remove her wide-brimmed hat and boots. 'Surely Charlie should be doing the tidying up, though? That's what he's paid for.'

Her mother smoothed her silvery-blonde bob back behind her ears and shrugged. 'We had to let him go—at least on a daily basis. He'll still come every month to do the lawns for us. Now, come and sit down and we'll have a nice chat. I've got all the papers for you—there are some wonderful photographs—it was such a lovely wedding—my bridge girls haven't been able to stop talking about it.'

She took Briar's arm and led the way through the house.

'You let Charlie go?' Briar asked, stunned. 'But why? You're supposed to have the money for all the staff now. We'd only just managed to get him back.'

'I know, and I was disappointed, but your father thinks it's a good idea to keep economising after our close call. Seeing we were getting the hang of it. Cameron wants to invest what we'd otherwise spend so we build up a nest egg in case we need it. Don't you think that's wise?'

Briar raised her eyebrows. She guessed it was, though it didn't sound like her father at all. 'So long as you don't end up doing all the work yourself.'

'Don't worry, Cameron's assured me of that.' She entered the kitchen. 'Now, what can I get you? Coffee or tea? I'm just about to have a cup of tea myself. And have you had lunch?'

'Tea would be great, thanks. And I could certainly do with a sandwich. Is Mavis around?'

Her mother pressed her lips together and sighed. 'Not till dinner time. We've cut her hours, too.'

'So who gets the meals?' Briar asked as her mother filled the kettle and turned it on. 'Not you, surely? You hate cooking. You always have.'

Carolyn rested a hand on her daughter's arm. 'I know, but I can make toast and cut a sandwich and it just seemed an extravagance we could do without.'

'And the shopping? And the washing? And the cleaning? Mavis was more than just a cook. She was the housekeeper.'

'I've been getting groceries delivered!' her mother exclaimed with a brightness that seemed less than sincere. 'Do you realise how convenient that is?'

Briar opened a canister and spooned some tea into a pot as her mother put together a couple of sandwiches while they waited for the kettle to boil.

'I think I'd better have a word with Dad. It's one thing to econ-omise, but I know how stressful it was before. Is he around?'

'No, he's out somewhere, I forget the details.'

Briar picked up on a frown her mother probably hadn't realised she'd given. 'Is everything all right? With Dad, I mean?'

'I think so. He's just out such a lot lately. Trying to re-estab-lish connections or network or some such. I don't know. Anyway, I don't know if it will do you any good at all to talk to him. He seems very determined to keep a tight rein on the money this time. He talks about it constantly. Anyway, how about we head for the conservatory where it's warm and bright and catch up with all your news? You must have so much to tell!'

That was one way of putting it, thought Briar as she carried a tray with the tea things through. But how much would her mother really want to hear? And wherever would she start?

'So,' her mother said, 'how was the honeymoon? I must say, I'm surprised to see you back quite so quickly. I had an idea Diablo was planning on staying away longer.'

Briar raised her eyebrows. Clearly Diablo had filled her parents in on their travel arrangements. She must have been the only one kept in the dark. 'He had to return suddenly for business. I'll write the phone number down for you.'

'Such a shame,' her mother said, sipping her tea. 'And did you have a good time? You looked awfully pale at your wedding. Everyone said so. So it's good to see you've got some colour in your cheeks again.'

'Weddings are supposed to be stressful, aren't they? I was bound to be pale.'

The older woman smiled and picked up a sandwich before leaning back in her cane chair, where the fronds of patted palms danced upon her shoulders. 'I seem to remember feeling that way, yes. Still, it doesn't take long to settle into married life and then you can't imagine not being married.'

'I don't know,' Briar confessed, studying the sandwich in her own hands as if it held all the answers. 'There's still so much I don't know about Diablo. I think it might take me some time to settle into this marriage, if I ever do.'

'Of course you will! And, if it helps, I didn't know your father very well when we married either. And here we are, thirty-five years later, still married.'

Briar looked up. 'I thought you two had known each other for years.'

'Well, we did, in passing. Our parents moved in the same circles of course, so we would often attend the same functions, but it was actually our fathers who thought we'd be a good match and brought us together.'

'What? You told me you met Dad at a party.'

'We did, but it was our fathers' doing.'

'They arranged your marriage?'

She laughed. 'Oh, that makes it sound so medieval. It wasn't like that at all. Although my parents thought it made sense, me being the only child and heir. Of course, they wanted me to marry well.'

'I don't believe it! And you went along with it?'

'I didn't even realise what was happening for a while—neither of us did. I just thought it was a coincidence that Cameron and I kept bumping into each other. I didn't realise that our fathers were pulling all the strings. And, I have to tell you, Cameron was a very good-looking young man. It was no hardship at all being with him. In no time at all they'd announced our engagement and that was that.'

That was that.

Briar could sympathise. She'd gone from single to married in what felt like sixty seconds. But her mother had never acted like a woman who'd been dragged kicking and screaming against her will into the marriage bed.

'But you love him,' she argued. 'You've always loved Dad.'

Her mother's eyes glistened with moisture. 'That grew. It wasn't love at first sight or anything. That took time. And I know it doesn't work for everyone, but having you and Nathaniel helped tremendously to bond us together.'

Her mother's eyes misted over and Briar reached out a hand to hers.

'Diablo wants us to have a baby. As soon as possible.'

She was rewarded with a wide smile. 'How wonderful! I'm so pleased.'

'Don't get too excited. I don't really know if I'm ready to have children yet.' *Let alone with Diablo.*

'Nonsense,' her mother retorted. 'You've always wanted to have children at some stage. And it's wise not to put it off for too long. Have them while you're young and energetic to run around after them, I think.' She sipped her tea and contemplated her daughter thoughtfully over the rim. 'Do you think Diablo will make a good father?'

Briar sighed. It wasn't something she'd wanted to think about, not given their circumstances, and yet it was a question she seemed to have more than enough material already to confuse her stance. 'I don't know. I mean, I'm not sure—it seems a huge step. We hardly know each other and it seems just silly to bring a baby into the equation when we've still so much to learn. But children seem to mean a lot to him and he is kinder than I ever thought possible—and generous. Did you have any idea he supports an entire school in Chile?'

'Well—' her mother leaned forward and replaced her now empty cup on her saucer '—it seems to me you're already softening your ideas towards Diablo. I know how rushed your wedding plans must have seemed, but do you see how quickly these feelings develop? I think you might already be falling for your new husband.'

Briar shook her head. 'Oh, no. I don't think so. I just think we were stuck together in the same house for a few days and I started to see his point of view on a few things. It's exactly the same as when hijackers take hostages who over time start to sympathise with their captors. That's all. We have nothing in common. Nothing.'

Her mother laughed. 'You should listen to yourself. You sound so melodramatic! You have nothing in common? So things aren't working out, say, in the bedroom department? If Diablo's thinking children, they'd want to be.'

The younger woman blinked at her mother, feeling herself flush. 'Um, that all…seems fine.'

Her mother sighed. 'Good. You know, when this marriage proposal scheme first came up, I was so worried for you. Diablo seemed, well, so mysterious and determined, and I know how these Mediterranean men can be quite…demanding, if you know what I mean.'

Briar cleared her throat. How did one tell one's mother that the sex with one's husband was mind-blowingly good? 'It's fine,' she repeated instead.

Her mother hardly seemed to notice. 'Mind you,' she continued, 'I felt a lot better when I saw the way he looks at you. It's quite clear he's besotted with you.'

It was Briar's turn to laugh. 'I don't think so. If there's one thing I know about Diablo, he doesn't do besotted. I suspect that when he looks at me he merely sees just one more possession in his ever-expanding portfolio.'

Her mother raised an eyebrow pointedly. 'You think so? Then, in that case, it's up to you to change that perception. Let him get to know you better, talk to him. You'll soon have him falling in love with you, just like you're beginning to fall in love with him.'

'You have to stop saying that! Don't you remember what he did to Dad? What he did to all of us? We were almost ruined and all because of him. How could anyone think I could ever love someone who was so ruthless?'

'He's a businessman—'

'That doesn't excuse what he did!'

'Maybe not, but he didn't have to help us get us back on our feet either.'

'Hardly out of the generosity of his heart.'

'Besides which, who we fall in love with isn't always within our control, however much we'd like to think it is.'

Briar had no comeback for that one but she still didn't believe it. Falling in love had never been on her agenda. Having Diablo's babies, likewise. If that suddenly changed, then how would she ever extricate herself from this mess of a marriage?

Falling in love with Diablo would ruin all her plans. How could she leave him if she loved him? And yet how could she stay when she knew she'd never be more than one more of his precious possessions?

'Look, if I was falling in love with Diablo,' she reasoned, immediately wondering why she was even bothering to pose the question, 'then wouldn't I know it? But all I feel lately is confused. I don't even know my own mind any more.'

Her mother picked up Briar's hands between her own. 'And what do you think falling in love feels like? It's like losing yourself, feeling alternately confused, excited, happy, never knowing whether to laugh or cry with happiness and frequently doing both. But you never really lose yourself. Sure, you abandon being a free agent, but what you gain from being in love is worth so much more.'

'But it's too soon! We've been married no time at all. It can't happen that quickly. Not when you don't even like the person!'

Her mother arched an eyebrow. 'But is that true? You really don't like Diablo?'

Of course! she wanted to shout. I don't like Diablo—I hate

him. But the words wouldn't come. Even though she wanted them to. Even though they had indeed been true once. She had detested the man, despised him, hated him with a passion.

But now the truth had changed. She didn't hate him at all— not really. She couldn't even say she disliked him. Hatred, dislike, had been replaced by another force. Her mind wandered back to his goodbye kiss at the door—that one soul-shattering kiss that had seemed to rip her soul from her and take it with him when he left. There was no way she could pretend she hated him after that. No. Loathing had been flushed out by another more potent force. She *wanted* him, plain and simple. And right now that was all she was prepared to admit to.

'It doesn't make sense,' Briar protested, disbelieving, the foundations of her life seeming to quake beneath her.

'We're talking about love,' her mother said, patting her on the hands. 'It's not supposed to make sense. Now, would you like some more tea? You look like you could use it.'

Briar let herself into the apartment, worried that Diablo would be angry she'd stayed out so late. She hadn't meant to, but by the time she'd finished talking to her mother and helped her dead-head the rest of the garden once the rain had eased, she was much later than she'd planned getting to the supermarket, which meant she'd hit the peak hour traffic on the way home. The fact most of it was going in the opposite direction was the only salvation.

But it had given her plenty of thinking time, which was what she'd needed—time to digest her mother's words and time to apply them to her own beleaguered thoughts.

When she'd gone into this marriage she'd expected she'd feel the same way about Diablo at the end of it as at the beginning. And yet, even after just a few days, her feelings towards her new husband were changing. And if she'd gone from out-and-out hatred to wanting him in that short space of time, what more could happen in a year or two?

'I'm home!' she called out, to nothing but the answering hum of a hungry refrigerator.

So he wasn't back yet. For once, a stroke of luck. She shrugged her overflowing bags of groceries down in the kitchen and dashed off to shower and get changed. Ten minutes later she was back, having changed her jeans and boots for a flirty layered skirt and fitted off-the-shoulder top. She'd pulled back the top section of her hair into a clip, leaving the rest to float around her shoulders. It was a style that made her feel feminine without impeding her in the kitchen.

She sorted the groceries, arranged the ingredients she'd need for dinner and set about organising a venue. The tombstone-filled dining room wouldn't do at all, but the tiny breakfast setting on one wall of the kitchen would be nicely intimate. She adorned it with a new chequered tablecloth, bold in blue and gold, set two new candle-holders with honey-coloured candles in the midst and set two places. She'd suspected his flatware would be expensive, white and unadorned and she'd been right, so she was glad she'd picked up napkins to complement the tablecloth and add more colour.

She stood back, surveying her work. It looked good. Cheerful. Inviting. Although it still lacked something…

With a spike of inspiration, she dashed up the stairs and found the bag of shells she'd tucked away in her case that morning. They were perfect. A perfect reminder of that day they'd really connected, a perfect reminder of how that day had ended. Maybe he might forgive her a little for her snippiness if he understood how much that day had meant to her?

She set them down between the candles and a raffia-covered bottle of Chianti she'd bought and uncorked in preparation, and set about preparing a simple dinner of spaghetti marinara with salad and garlic bread. Mussel soup and an Italian grocery shop-bought cassata would complete the meal. It wasn't a Spanish menu, but she knew he loved Italian food and, with any luck, she'd have it all ready by the time he came back.

Maybe tonight they could talk. Maybe she could explain to him how confused she'd been feeling. Maybe she'd have a chance to let him know that she'd like to become more than just a possession to him.

By eight o'clock she had everything ready, an inch away from simmering, a few moments away from serving. Breathing a sigh of relief, she checked her make-up, removed her apron and allowed herself half a glass of Chianti. After all, if she was going to tell Diablo half the things she expected to tonight, she could do with a dollop of intestinal fortitude along the way.

By nine o'clock she'd drained her glass and had resorted to reading a magazine she'd found in the living room.

By ten o'clock she'd exhausted the magazine and flipped through every cable channel going, still finding nothing to hold her interest—not when one question dominated her thoughts. Where was he? He'd told her he wouldn't be too late. Was this Diablo's idea of not late? Or did he simply not care?

Which gave way to the ugliest thought of them all. Maybe the important meeting he'd rushed back for was nothing to do with business after all? Maybe he'd needed time with a lover to atone for the time spent with his irrational wife?

And just because he'd never been photographed with the same woman twice didn't mean a man like Diablo wouldn't have a lover stashed away somewhere discreet. He'd obviously had plenty of lovers before her appearance on the scene—why should that change now, simply because he was married? He probably couldn't wait to rekindle old flames.

But then he'd kissed her when he'd left the apartment. Was he that cruel, to go straight from her arms to a lover's?

And how could she really blame him if he *had* sought sanctuary in another's arms?

No. She couldn't blame him. But that didn't stop her wanting to strangle whoever he was with!

At eleven, she flipped through the phone book, looking for Diablo's office number, annoyed she hadn't yet loaded his phone numbers into her mobile. No rush, she'd thought—when was she ever likely to want to call him? She dialled the number for his office and unsurprisingly received an after hours message. 'Leave your message after the beep,' the machine instructed. *Where are you?* she was tempted to ask. But he should be here long before he ever got such a message. And what would he make of a message like that? Would he think his distant wife had suddenly turned into a clinging vine?

She circled the kitchen, checking out a soup that was past its best and putting a lid on the tomato sauce she had already prepared, waiting for Diablo to walk through the door so she could add the seafood. The fresh pasta sat ready next to its pot, waiting for him to come so she could boil the water. Waiting. Everything pointlessly waiting. She checked the time once more and decided that, even if he came home now, he would have already eaten.

Almost midnight. Diablo clearly wasn't coming home this side of tomorrow. And the irony of the situation almost made her laugh out loud. That on the very day she'd started admitting to herself that she wanted her husband, and that she'd seriously started entertaining ideas that maybe she was falling in love with him, she'd already lost him. He didn't even care enough to come home so she could tell him!

She wanted to be angry. She wanted to rail against the sheer injustice of it all. She wanted to leave and find herself a bed in some anonymous hotel—somewhere where Diablo wouldn't find her.

But what was the point? If he didn't come home, he'd never

appreciate her token gesture. And, instead of anger, all she felt was a bone weariness that sapped her of all energy.

She took one last look around the kitchen before she snapped off the lights and headed upstairs to bed. She wasn't hungry anyway.

It had been a bitch of a night. Diablo let himself into the darkened apartment hours later than he'd intended, looking forward to nothing more than drinking a beer and going to bed. And if Briar had any sense, she was already tucked up, fast asleep. Given her mood lately, it was probably just as well. He wasn't in the mood for little Miss Snippy right now and, with what he had to tell her, it was better she had a full night's sleep first. He rolled his neck from side to side. *Dios*, he was tired.

Enough light filtered through the blinds that he could make his way to the refrigerator without turning on a light. Besides, the tempting smell of garlic coming from that direction was enough to lure him. Briar must have organised herself a pizza. With any luck there might be a piece or two left over. His stomach growled at the prospect.

He pulled open the fridge door and blinked at overflowing shelves of smallgoods and vegetables, a covered salad and what looked like a plate of uncooked seafood.

He stepped back, the light from the fridge illuminating more than the usual empty benchtops. With a frown he let the door go and snapped on the down lights, taking in the pans on the hot-plates and the pasta still in its bag nearby. But it was the table, set for an intimate dinner for two, that stopped him in his tracks.

'What the...?' He wandered over, looking at the table, the Chianti, a tablecloth he didn't recognise and candles. He picked up one of the shells, curling his fingers around it, weighing it lightly in his hands. Briar had cooked him dinner? He'd half thought she'd merely been being contrary. He sure hadn't expected this. But she'd obviously been expecting him.

He flipped the shell over in his hand, and then he flipped it again. He'd meant to call. And then he'd got caught up and suddenly it had been too late. Not that he'd thought she'd give a damn anyway. She hadn't seemed too thrilled to be with him at all today. *Yesterday*, he corrected himself.

He looked around the kitchen. Obviously she had given a damn if she'd gone to this much trouble. Who knew?

He climbed the stairs to the bedroom, surprised to find the light in the *en suite* bathroom still on. Had she left it on for him or had it been for her own benefit, her first night in a new home? The light spilled across her face and her hair that ribboned across the pillow. He frowned and looked closer. A shadow marred her pillow where there should be none. He looked closer, touching the pads of his fingertips lightly to the area. Moisture? Had she cried herself to sleep? Something inside him yawned open and, for the first time since his mother died, he felt himself wanting something he couldn't have.

If only he could get a handle on what it was.

He stood there for a long time, looking down at the sleeping form of his wife—his beautiful wife, his complex wife.

What was tonight's dinner meant to represent? A peace offering? Or merely the latest tactic in her hot and cold war?

He doubted she even knew herself.

One thing was for sure—after going to that much trouble she wasn't likely to be in a good mood when she woke up. Which made what he had to tell her even more difficult.

He unbuttoned his shirt as he made for the *en suite* bathroom. *Dios*, what a mess.

The unfamiliar sound of a telephone ringing wrenched her from her dreams. Strange dreams. Uncomfortable dreams. Dreams filled of loss and sadness and yet the sensation of heat and strong arms around her. But, just the same as she'd gone to sleep, she woke up alone.

Maybe not so alone, she suddenly realised, her scratchy eyes registering the indentation in the pillow beside her, her ears registering the play of water and muted hum of the exhaust fan from the *en suite* bathroom in between the ring tones.

What time had Diablo come back?

She blinked and made a stab for the phone, lifting it from its cradle. 'Hello?'

Through the sobs she recognised her mother's voice. 'Oh, Briar, I'm so glad it's you. We've had such dreadful news and I don't know what to do.'

CHAPTER ELEVEN

ADRENALINE powering her senses to red alert, Briar sat bolt upright in bed. 'What's wrong? What's happened?'

'Your father had a meeting with Diablo last night. He's cut us off totally. No more allowance. No more money. We've still got the house for now but I don't know how we're going to manage.'

'But why?' Briar asked, trying to form a picture of whatever had transpired last night. Diablo had met her father? Was that where he'd been all that time? With her father and not with a woman? Nothing made sense. 'I don't understand.'

'Neither do I. I thought we were managing so well. And I'm worried about your father—he only came home a few hours ago and he seems so agitated and, well, frankly I'm worried about him.'

'There has to be a mistake. Diablo can't do that. The agreement…'

'Cameron said the agreement was off.'

Air hissed through Briar's teeth. 'And did Dad say why?'

'Oh dear, Cameron was very upset. I don't think—'

'Tell me,' she insisted, her fingers tightening around the phone.

Her mother sobbed again. 'Cameron said Diablo didn't need him any more. That he'd got what he wanted.'

Her eyes turned in the direction of the *en suite* bathroom.

Bastard, she told him in a mental blast that should have melted a path clear through the walls. *You total bastard!*

'Do you think you can talk to him? Do you think you can do any good?'

Briar was already out of bed, scrabbling for clothes, determined to get dressed before Diablo emerged from the bathroom. 'He's not going to get away with this. Don't worry. I'll sort something out. I'll be right over, okay?'

Briar pulled on jeans and a sweater, each item donned to the accompaniment of a curse, all of them directed squarely at Diablo. She was just pulling her hair into a rough ponytail when the subject of her cursing appeared, one low-slung towel casually knotted at hip level, while he dried off his hair with another, his satiny skin still glistening from the steam.

He stopped in the open doorway, the hand rubbing his hair slowing to a halt. 'You're awake, then.'

She turned her head away, raising an eyebrow as she plonked herself down on the bed to pull on her boots. 'Your powers of observation astonish me.'

Out of her peripheral vision she saw him walk to the wardrobe, pulling open one door. 'So you are angry with me. I thought you might be.'

'Of course I'm bloody angry with you! What the hell did you expect?'

'I didn't realise it was so important.'

'You broke your word. You lied to me.'

He groaned and turned. 'Don't you think you're overreacting just a little? I was prepared to apologise, but now I see that would merely be pointless.'

'You think an apology would make up for what you've done? You've got some nerve.'

'Then what do you want?'

'To get the hell out of here.'

'You're leaving because I didn't call?'

'What the hell are you talking about?' she demanded, facing up to him.

'I had no idea you'd go to so much trouble.' He continued to look at her as if she were mad. 'Dinner. Candles. A table set for two.'

She waved his words away with a slash of her hand.

'I'm not talking about last night.'

His chest expanded on a deep breath. 'Then, to use your own eloquent words—what the hell *are* you talking about?'

'My mother just called. She told me you're reneging on the agreement. No more funds, no more cash.'

He dumped the towel he was holding on to the floor. 'Ah. Then you've heard.'

'Oh, yes, I've heard it all. I've heard how you gave my father the happy news, telling him the "gravy-train" was over now that you've got your polite society wife in the bag.'

His eyes glistened, suddenly merciless. 'Well, that's a blatant lie for a start. Nobody would ever make the mistake of calling you a polite society wife—least of all me.'

Briar squeezed her hands into fists. If that comment was supposed to support his defence, he was way off base. She pulled open the wardrobe door, yanking out the bag she'd unpacked just last night and slamming it down with a thump on the wide bed.

'So don't I at least get the chance to defend myself?'

'Sure.' She unzipped the bag and looked at him. 'Did you or did you not tell my father you were cutting off their funds—the funds you promised when you married me?'

His eyes narrowed, hardened, glistening like stone. 'I did.'

She flipped the bag open. 'Then that's all the confirmation I need. If your deal with him is off, then your deal with me is off, too. I no longer am required to be your wife. I guess we'll all breathe a sigh of relief about that.'

She made a move towards the wardrobe but he stepped in front of her, his legs planted wide, his arms crossed over that bare chest and with the towel lashed around his hips looking like an ancient Egyptian god painted on a wall—tall, proud and disapproving. Except this man was far from being some two dimensional painting. Even now she could feel the heat coming from him, the air crisp and crackling with electricity around him.

'You don't get out of being my wife that easily.'

'Maybe you should have thought of that,' she said, glaring up at him, 'before you pulled the pin on this agreement. You can hardly expect me to stay married to you after this. I can't believe that even you could be so callous, especially after everything my father was doing to make a new start. You probably don't have any idea how hard he's been working—trying to find ways of saving money—economising.'

The statue in front of her frowned. 'Economising—how?'

'I knew you wouldn't realise,' she said dismissively. 'Dad thought it a good idea to save some money. He figured they'd managed for so long without every convenience that they could get by with less household help. He was saving the rest for a nest egg. And now that you've pulled the pin, it's just as well he's set something aside to invest.'

Diablo snarled, his lip curling. 'Oh, he "invested" it, I have no doubt. What I do doubt is that there is any such "nest egg" to fall back on, given the type of investments your father prefers are generally the "double or nothing" variety.'

'What are you saying?'

'Just that if he's been running to form, he's probably already gambled it away.'

'You're insane! You don't know when to give up.'

She sidestepped around him and opened the wardrobe door, reaching in for the few items she'd unpacked only last night.

'And where do you think this meeting I had with your father took place last night? At the local church hall?'

'You tell me. You're the one making the accusations here.'

'At a very private, very select gaming club. In fact, the fourth I'd tracked him down to…'

She shrugged. She hadn't known her father ever went to such places, but what of it? 'He's over eighteen; it's hardly illegal. So what were you doing there?'

'Trying to stop him.'

That pulled her head around. 'From what?'

'From gambling all that was left of the money I had transferred to his account on our wedding day.'

'I don't believe you. You want to renege on the deal you made with my parents and now you're trying to find a way to pin it on my father.'

'Your father is a gambler. He promised me when we made this deal that he'd stay out of the gambling dens.'

'Why should I believe you?'

'Think about it. Why else do you think his interests made for such easy pickings? Because he'd already gambled away their cash flow.'

'Because you stole it out from under him!'

'No—because, no matter what his status, your father is not the world's sharpest businessman.' He cut off her protest before she could put voice to it. 'Competent, sure, but Cameron Davenport is no world-beater in the business stakes. He'd been losing money for years. It didn't matter for a long time—there was plenty to lose. But when it did start to matter, he found himself a way of replacing what he'd lost. Or that was the plan.'

'I don't know why I'm even listening to this.'

'Because it's the truth and you need to hear it! But, God knows I didn't want to be the one to tell you.'

'Don't give me that. You're enjoying this. You've always wanted what my father had—the place in society he occupied, his moneyed connections. And now you've got all that—and me— it's still not enough. You have to pull him down to rock bottom.'

'I didn't want this!'

'I don't believe you.' She zipped up the only half-filled bag and jerked it off the bed. 'This is exactly the way I expected you to behave, given your reputation. I don't know why I ever trusted you.'

'And just where do you think you're going with that bag?'

'Somewhere I should have gone last night. I'm going home. *My home.*'

'And what do you think that will achieve?'

'It will get me away from you, for a start. Besides, my parents need me now.'

'So you're going back to dear old Dad?'

'At least he loves me!'

His eyes narrowed, one dark eyebrow arched pointedly. 'Are you sure this has nothing to do with last night? A prepared meal—a table set for two? What were you hoping to achieve—some kind of declaration of love eternal?'

'From you? Hardly!' she exclaimed, and at least that much was the truth. 'I couldn't give a damn about last night!' She pulled up the handle on her bag and started for the door, the prick of tears stinging her eyes. 'It's about being there for people—people who love you. You wouldn't understand.'

'Oh, yeah,' he said, a cruel tilt sullying his perfect mouth, 'I understand perfectly. Like the daddy who loves his sweet daughter so much he gambled her away in a hand of blackjack.'

Her head snapped around and she took one final look at the man she'd been married to for little more than ten minutes and yet which felt emotionally like ten lifetimes. 'And that's your last desperate attempt to justify what you've done?' She shook her head slowly from side to side. Was there no end to the ways he could twist the truth to his own purposes? Did he forget she'd been there that night in her father's study when this deal had been put together?

And to think she'd felt stirrings of jealousy that he might

have been with another woman. To think that she'd even imagined she was starting to fall in love with him! She'd even been dreaming of having his babies! Thank God they'd never had that chance to talk last night. That she'd never revealed how she felt. How much more stupid would she feel today if she had?

Because she couldn't love him. There was no chance of that—especially not now. This empty ache she felt inside was merely a cold gaping slash of betrayal, growing ever larger when she realised how close she'd come to laying down her heart for him.

'I hate you,' she spat at him. 'I never realised how much until now. I never want to see you again.'

'And when you discover I'm telling the truth, what happens then? Don't expect to come crawling back.'

'Not a chance,' she said. *'On both counts.'*

'So you're leaving me.'

'What was I just saying about those powers of observation?'

'In spite of our contract?'

'I'd say that particular pile of trash doesn't count for much right now, wouldn't you?'

'And if you're pregnant?' he called out behind her.

She stopped, breathed in deep and twisted around. 'Look Diablo—'

'And don't tell me about how unlikely it is. There's still a chance.'

If only you knew, she thought, thanking the heavens there was no risk of that happening to further complicate matters.

'How about we just cross that bridge *if* we come to it?'

Normally the drive out of the city relaxed him—leaving the city behind, heading for the seclusion of the coast and the fresh sea air. Not today.

Today his stomach was tied in knots, his mind tangled with unfinished business.

And that annoyed the hell out of him.

Because she'd gone. The woman who'd driven him crazy with not knowing what she wanted had made her choice and walked out of his life. The fact it was the wrong choice was her problem. But, instead of feeling as if a weight had been lifted from his shoulders, he felt as if an anvil had been implanted inside his chest.

She'd walked out on him. And at the time he'd been happy to let her go. He didn't need the endless sparring. He wouldn't miss the aggravation. And, if she wanted to believe her father over him, then what could he do? Even when—*if*—she pressed Cameron for the truth, would he tell her? Or would he be satisfied to let Diablo take the rap for everything that had gone wrong—just like before?

How he could have looked Diablo in the face last night and deny he had a problem when he'd all but gambled his life down the toilet, he didn't know.

All he did know was that it had been pointless trying to work in the office. It had been worse in the apartment. The cleaner had been thorough, eradicating all trace of food from last night's aborted dinner attempt, but still the cloth remained on the table, the candles and shells gaily adorning the chequered fabric, the fridge full of food she'd never cook.

Briar had made him dinner. Just like a real wife. A thin smile forced its way to his lips. A *real* wife. How about that?

The smile dissolved as he accelerated through a bend. No doubt she'd be stuck with making meals for her parents now. Because with their funds exhausted, the cook would be certain to go, and the cleaner and all the other assorted household help. Briar would no doubt end up doing the lion's share, a poor little Cinderella. Only this Cinderella would have neither a fairy godmother nor the happy ending she'd been so keen to advocate.

So be it. Maybe then she'd believe what he'd been telling her. He steered the car on to the road leading to El Paradiso.

No happy ending. That was no surprise. He'd never expected one. It was just a waste that it had had to finish this way.

She found her mother in tears, slumped on a stool at the kitchen bench. 'Briar!' she cried, falling into her arms like a bag of bones. 'Your father locked himself in the study after he came home and he refuses to come out. I'm so worried about him.'

Oh, God, Briar prayed, *please don't let him do anything crazy*. She massaged her mother's back, trying to soothe her before she went in search of her father, while inwardly she churned with fear for all of them. How desperate must her father be feeling right now?

'I'll go to him. He'll talk to me. He has to.' And if he didn't she'd call someone—an ambulance, the police, even the fire brigade—anyone who could knock the door down.

Her mother looked up suddenly, her features pinched and her voice desperate. 'Did you talk to Diablo? What did he say?'

How could she tell her? A spike of anger lanced her fears. *Damn Diablo and his broken promises. Damn him for his callous accusations.*

'I've left him, Mum. I'm not going back.'

Her mother let her go, her red-rimmed eyes wide with shock. Then she cradled her daughter's face with her hands.

'Oh, Briar, no.'

She covered her mother's hands with her own and pulled them slowly away between her own. 'I had no choice. I couldn't stay with him, not after this.'

'But there must be some explanation, something we can do. You can't throw what you've got away.'

'No. I've decided. And right now I have more important things to worry about, like seeing if Dad's okay. Now, maybe you could knock up a couple of sandwiches? I bet Dad hasn't eaten for ages.'

Bare minutes later, she knocked on the study door. 'Dad, it's me.' She waited a few seconds, then tested the handle. Locked, just as her mother had told her.

'Dad, are you okay?'

'I don't want to see anyone.'

Relief flooded through her at his voice. She leaned her forehead against the timber. 'Please let me in. I need to talk to you.'

Seconds passed—long, silent seconds that seemed to stretch for ever, and then she heard it, the metallic click of the key grating in the lock.

She held her breath just a few seconds longer before trying the handle again. This time it turned and she let herself into the room. It was dark, the blinds drawn, no lights on and at first it was difficult to see anything. Her nostrils twitched. The air was heavy with the combined aroma of stale cigar smoke and malt whiskey, overlaid with a blanket of absolute despair. Even the ticking of the grandfather clock seemed oppressive. But it wasn't the room, she realised, it was her father's desperation colouring the air, as his body slumped into the chair behind his desk, his forehead resting on his hands.

'Dad,' she said, 'I've been so worried about you.'

He lifted his head and, even in the dimness, she could see the haggard lines that marred his features and the red-lipped rims pulling down from his eyes.

'Briar.' His voice came as a croak. 'What are we to do?'

She tried to smile. 'We'll work something out. We always do.'

He sighed and held out a hand to her. 'What would we all do without you?'

She circled the desk and took his hand, squeezing it, before kissing him on the cheek and sitting down at his feet, resting her arm on his knee just as she'd done when she was a little girl and had just wanted to be with him. 'I bet I could still get that job at the gallery if I wanted it.'

He touched her chin, lifting it around. 'You shouldn't have to do that.'

'I don't mind helping. We have to do something.'

'I don't deserve you. And you certainly deserve a better father than me.'

'Rubbish.'

He shook his head. 'You shouldn't be thinking about getting a job. You have your own future to think about. You have another life—a married life.'

She shook her head, praying it wouldn't shake loose the tears that were suddenly so close to falling.

'Not any more. I've left him.'

'My God. I've ruined everything.'

'No, you didn't ruin anything. Diablo did that when he reneged on the contract. I hate him for what he's done. And I hate myself more for ever trusting him. I should have seen this coming. Maybe I could have stopped him. Maybe I could have done something...'

'Briar—'

'...but at least things can get back to normal, even if we might be a bit broke. It's just so good to be home with you both. We'll manage. I know we will.'

'Briar,' her father said more strongly this time, 'you have to listen to me.'

She looked up at him. 'What is it?'

'You can't leave Diablo.'

'Of course I can. He reneged on the deal. He broke the contract. I'll make an appointment with our lawyers. They'll find some way out of this.'

'Diablo didn't break the terms of the contract.'

His words silenced her, fear gripping her heart as Diablo's accusations leached back into her mind. But Diablo had been lying—hadn't he? 'What do you mean?'

'*I* broke the contract. Diablo was only doing what he'd promised me he would. I was too stupid to believe he wouldn't.

And I was stupid enough to think I'd get away with it. I thought you were still up on the North Coast. I thought he'd never find out. One decent winning streak, I thought…'

'Oh, Dad. No…'

'And I was winning, for a while,' he whispered, his eyes staring blindly ahead in the gloomy study. 'Just one more bet, I told myself, just one more and really clean up and show Carolyn and you that I wasn't worthless, that I didn't have to rely on Diablo's handouts. But I lost. And then I had to have one more bet to get back what I'd lost. And then another. But I kept losing. And that's when Diablo found me.'

Her thoughts in turmoil, her emotions in tatters, Briar battled to make sense of her father's admission, the crippling realisation that Diablo had been right.

'Mum told me you'd cut back on home help to economise—but you were using the money for their wages to gamble, weren't you?'

Her father fixed his desperate gaze on to her. 'It's true. And do you know what the worst thing was? I was too stupid, even then, to admit that I had a problem.'

'Oh, Dad.' She squeezed his hand as the first tears squeezed from her eyes and she knew that the worst thing had been calling Diablo a liar. She'd told him she hated him because of it. Given that she loved him, *what did that make her?*

'I've been sitting here all morning,' her father continued, 'blaming Diablo for everything. I came in here to work out how I was going to get back at him, but the longer I thought about it, the more I realised it wasn't Diablo's fault at all. I'm the one to blame. I'm the one responsible. I've wagered away an entire fortune and a half and I was willing to let Diablo take the blame for everything.'

'It's not all your fault. If he hadn't pursued the takeover so ruthlessly…'

'He did what he had to do. He saw a weakness and he took

advantage. Of course I hung it all on him, badmouthing him to everyone who would listen. It was easier than admitting that I was a failure.'

'You're not a failure!'

'I've lost a fortune along with my own and my wife's sizeable inheritances. What should I call myself?' He set his bloodshot eyes on hers. 'I tried to tell you, on your wedding day. I wanted you to know it was all my fault, that I was sorry.'

She blinked, thinking back to that day, when her father had seemed the one who needed calming, the one who needed reassurance.

'You did try,' she said, nodding. 'I remember. But tell me, what happens now?'

'I'm going to get help this time. I promised Diablo weeks ago that I would and I never followed up on it. I should have. Today I'm going to do it.'

'Then I'll come with you,' she said.

'No,' he said firmly. 'Your place is with your husband.'

She turned her head away, not wanting to think about the mess she'd left behind this morning and the man at the centre of it. He'd said such horrible things—inexcusable things. Even if he'd had to reveal her father's gambling, he hadn't had to twist the knife by suggesting he could gamble his own daughter away. 'I don't think I have a husband any more.'

He tilted her face around until she was looking up at him. 'You should go to him. Don't let your marriage fall apart because of my weakness. I have enough on my conscience without that, too.'

'I want to stay with you—help you.'

'And don't think I don't appreciate it, child. But I'm the last person in the world who deserves your support.'

'That's not true! You're my father.'

'It's more than true. I know you were railroaded into this

marriage, but I knew Diablo would make you a good husband.
I would never have let you go to someone I didn't respect.'

'I thought you hated him.'

'I did, for his skills and his business acumen and because he's
one hundred times the businessman I am—in fact, all the very
reasons I respect him.

'But then he proved himself beyond that. He knew you would
hardly be overjoyed at your marriage, whatever the reason, so
he let everyone think he was to blame for our circumstances,
saving you and Carolyn from discovering my sad secret. And
then he let you believe he had paid for you, to protect you from
the ugliest secret of them all.'

She rose to her knees, her hands on his arm, imploring. 'What
do you mean?'

'Our arrangement, for Diablo to marry you in return for
money and this property, wasn't quite as it seemed.'

Chills radiated from her core to her extremities, like tiny
icicles needling their way through her. 'No. You didn't. Please,
God, tell me you didn't…'

He squeezed his eyes shut. 'Briar, I'm so sorry. You were the
only thing I had left, the only thing worth something. Diablo told
me to stop, that I'd lost enough, but still I didn't listen. He already
had the house; he already had everything. But my luck had to
change so I ignored him. I told him I still had you—winner takes
all—and he told me I was a monster and that I was mad, but still
I played. And lost. I gambled with my daughter and I lost and
I'll never be able to forgive myself for it.'

'You wagered me away.'

She bit down on her lip, trying to staunch the tears, the tears
that found an echo in her father's eyes. They tracked a ragged
path down his stubble-covered cheeks as the clock chimes
sounded out the hour.

He sniffed and wiped his face with a handkerchief. 'Diablo

came up with the plan to say he'd take you in settlement for the house. He didn't have to. He'd already won everything we had. I know he wanted a good marriage, but I suspect he felt sorry for me, and even more sorry for you.'

'I don't know what to say.'

'You don't have to say anything. It's me who has to make amends. The one good thing to come out of all this is that you married a good, strong man. He'll never make the mistakes I did. Can't you see? Your place is not with me, the man who gambled you away—your place is with Diablo. He's a good man. Go to him.'

Briar squeezed her father's hand. If only it were as simple as that. He'd asked her what she'd do when she found out he was telling the truth. He'd told her not to come crawling back. And her response came back in horrible wide screen detail. *'Not a chance,'* she'd asserted. *'On both counts.'*

And Diablo *had* been telling the truth.

And, if she wanted him back, she had no choice.

She was going to have to go crawling right back.

Just as soon as she worked out how…

CHAPTER TWELVE

BREATHING time. Briar needed breathing time to work out what she was going to do. An apology was the very least she owed him, but would he accept it from her, the way she'd stormed out on him? And beyond that... Beyond that was hope. If he would talk to her, maybe she could admit her mistakes, tell him how wrong she'd been. Tell him how she was willing to try again.

Tell him she loved him...

But until she worked out how, it was a good distraction to have her father's well-being to focus on, and making sure he carried out his commitment to change. Her mother took the news of her husband's addiction like a diagnosis that finally gave her a long-awaited answer. "It explains quite a lot," she said. "At least now we know what we're dealing with."

Then she'd located a counsellor they were all happy with and by the end of the day they'd all met and talked and mapped out a course of action. It wasn't going to be easy but with support her father could overcome his addiction.

It was late by the time they came home from the counsellor's and Briar could see her mother was exhausted. While half of her was desperate to see Diablo, the other half knew that her parents needed her more. Maybe by tomorrow, she told herself, Diablo would have had a chance to cool down and might be more receptive to her words. She could only hope.

So she fixed dinner for them all and spent the evening with them, sleeping that night in her old bed. It felt so strange to be back and yet it was barely a week before that she'd left to become a married woman. A married woman who now had an enormous problem. How to save her marriage when she'd been the one to so thoroughly assign it to the garbage bin.

She thought about calling, but what she had to say had to be said in person, so after a sleepless night she left early despite a foggy, aching head, determined to surprise Diablo before he left for work. But the apartment was empty and as cold as a grave, the dining room chairs chillingly taunting her in their two rigid lines. She rang his office only for his PA to tell her that Diablo was not available and wouldn't be for some time.

'Didn't I meet you at the wedding?' Briar cried desperately, recognising the PA's voice. 'Can't you tell me where he's gone? You have to tell me.'

The PA's tones softened and Briar felt pity coursing down the line; she was sorry, she said, but she couldn't reveal where he'd gone, least of all over the phone.

'I'll come down to his office,' Briar offered.

'I'm sorry,' answered the PA, before hanging up.

Briar flopped down in the kitchen at the tiny table where she'd planned to show Diablo that he hadn't made a mistake marrying her, feeling beaten, utterly defeated. Her hand drifted to the shells still lying there and she smiled as she remembered finding them. She picked one up and held it close, moving it, watching its pink lustre dance in the light.

They'd been happy for such a short time, just a few hours, but the memory of that one very special day made her heart swell. Those hours she'd been in Diablo's arms had been so magical, until she'd scared herself stupid with the realisation she might be falling in love with him. And then everything had gone pear-shaped. She'd sent them pear-shaped.

If only she had the chance to go back and make things better! She curled her hand around the shell as the random thought struck her.

Maybe…

On a hunch she raced to the phone and redialled Diablo's office. 'El Paradiso!' she cried, as soon as his PA answered. 'Is that where he's gone? Is that what you can't tell me?'

The PA hesitated. Then her voice softened. 'Please understand, I'm not telling you anything. But drive safely, Mrs Barrentes.'

Briar nervously pulled up at the security gates outside the house early in the afternoon and pressed the intercom button. Luisa answered, delighted to hear her voice, delighted to let her in.

She was under no misapprehension Diablo would share the same sentiments as she parked her car beside the entrance and with shaky knees made her way to the door. Halfway there it swung open and for a moment she smiled, expecting to see Luisa's broad face beaming a welcome. But it was someone much taller, much more daunting, who stared down at her now and shrank her smile right away, as the niggling headache that had been building behind her eyes all day turned suddenly blinding.

Diablo stood in the open doorway, looking every bit as dark and imposing as he had that first night at her house. How strange, she thought, that back then he'd been the one on the outside, the one seeking entry.

How the tables had turned.

'For someone who never wanted to see me again, you've driven a long way to do exactly the opposite.'

She swallowed, hard. 'I have to talk to you.'

'Why do you think I'd be interested in anything you have to say?'

She stole a breath, trying to unravel the speech she'd been rehearsing the entire journey from the roof of her mouth. But the speech was stuck fast there along with her tongue while blood pumped louder and angrier in her temples.

Diablo leaned into the doorway in his signature style, crossing his arms and legs. Even with his dark hair swinging loose around his face and dressed in a casual shirt and shorts the action carried with it an air of superiority. 'Well?'

The words of her planned speech dissolved in a feeling of overwhelming inferiority.

'I spoke to my father,' she blurted out instead. 'You were right—about everything. I'm sorry.'

A muscle twitched in his jaw.

'Is that it?'

'Diablo…' She took a step closer but he uncrossed his legs, suddenly growing taller and looking down at her so imperiously that she stopped. 'I know you must be disappointed with me. I'm sorry I didn't believe you, but how could I? It was just too horrible.'

'So you preferred to believe that it was me who could make up anything so horrible.'

She lifted both her hands. 'Of course I did. Why should that be such a surprise? You have to understand—'

'I understand! I knew what you thought about me when we married. I knew you weren't happy. But I thought that with time you might get to know me, and see that I am not such a monster as you believed. But you chose to paint me in the worst possible light every chance you got.'

'Then maybe if you'd been straight with me from the start things might have been different! But what was I supposed to believe when nobody told me the truth, treating me like some child who had to be protected from the truth? You cultivated my beliefs about you. You supported them. What hope did we have?'

'Obviously, none at all,' he said, flicking off her grievances like some annoying insect. He stared down at her, his eyes temporarily softening. 'It is my turn to apologise. I didn't think you needed to know all the sordid details of your father's deal.'

She gritted her teeth, hissing air between them before huffing it out. 'I know you were trying to protect us all from the truth, but I was bound to find out some time. And, when I did, how could I not feel bad about the whole deal? Don't you see that? What else was I supposed to think?'

He swiped a hand back through his hair, his eyes looking at a point somewhere over her head.

'I have no idea. Now, if that's all…?'

Panic seized her thoughts. He was trying to send her away?

'No, it's not all!' she protested. 'Dammit, but I will not be dismissed like some nameless messenger! I'm still your wife, after all.'

His eyebrows reacted to her words with a lazy hitch. 'A title you seemed to have major objections to only recently.'

She forced her shoulders back. 'I acted hastily. I don't deny it. But there were, you'll agree, extenuating circumstances. So I've decided I should give our marriage another go.'

His lip curled. *she'd decided.* She had some nerve. 'How do I know you won't change your mind again? You've been running hot and cold on me ever since our engagement.'

She looked up at him, her amber eyes marred with shadows. 'Because, in addition to learning the truth about my father and the dealings that brought us together, I've just discovered something that means I can't just walk away from this marriage.'

For just one instant his heart jumped in his chest—but just as quickly he damped down on the thought. There was no chance she was delivering the news he most wanted to hear from a wife.

'And that is?' he asked, already losing interest.

'I love you,' she blurted. 'I came to tell you that I love you.'

He laughed at his own folly. He'd been right in assuming it was nothing that really mattered.

'You love me?' he mocked, as she seemed to shrink before him. 'What is this? A last-ditch attempt to mount a rescue mission for your broke family—you're offering to sell yourself to me again? I warn you, the price would be nowhere near as generous as the first time around.'

'No! This has nothing to do with my family! This has to do with you and me. My parents don't even know I'm here. My father's getting himself sorted out. We spent yesterday finding him a counsellor and getting him some real help. He's determined to beat his addiction this time.'

'So you're not here for the money?'

'Why won't you listen to me? I'm here because I love you! God only knows it was the last thing I wanted to happen, but it did.'

'This from the woman who told me in no uncertain terms little more than a day ago that she hated me? And yet now who professes to love me?'

Her amber eyes flared and she crossed her arms over her chest. 'So I was angry.'

His eyes followed the movement, in spite of himself enjoying the swell of breasts outlined beneath her scoop-necked top and, even more, the sliver of stomach revealed as the hem hitched up. Last night he'd smelt her hair on his pillow, her scent on his sheets, and he'd ached long and hard, trying to get her out of his mind, without success. How much harder was it going to be tonight when he could imagine himself sliding his hand up that top and capturing those lush breasts? How much harder was *he* going to be?

'You get angry a lot,' he muttered, without returning his eyes to her face.

'So do you,' she rejoined, 'but I still love you in spite of it.'

Touché. He blinked, slowly, and slid his eyes back to her face. 'Nevertheless…a pointless endeavour.'

'Which means what exactly?'

'Which means I can't help you. I thought I'd already told you,

I believed we could make this marriage work but don't expect me to love you. Now I'm not even sure our marriage can work at all and so if you think you're going to put pressure on me to expect me to love you...'

She shook her head. *Too eagerly?* 'No,' she said, 'I can't change the way you feel, any more than I can change the way I do. But I'll take whatever you're offering—' She hesitated, looking suddenly unsure despite her earlier bravado. 'If you're still offering, that is.'

'Don't you remember?' he argued menacingly. 'You turned me down flat. You were the one who walked away.'

'I know.' She held out her hands to him. 'But I was wrong. Which is why I'm here now. Don't you understand what it took to come here?'

He let her stand there, waiting for his response. She'd walked out on him because she'd thought he'd lied to her, when in fact it was truth he'd actively hidden from the start. Could he really hold her accountable for walking out on him like she had, when he'd engineered the circumstances? Besides, he still burned for her. And she was right here, right now...

'So what exactly is it you want?'

'I want to be with you,' she whispered. 'I want to wake up with you every morning. I want to make love with you every night and every day. I want to be the mother of your children. I want the whole damn package.

'Don't you get it?' she implored when he didn't make any attempt to respond. 'It's not just about loving you—I *want* you. I don't want to live without you, and if you want me too, even if you don't love me, then that's enough for me.'

Something larger than a mere heart had to be pumping in his chest, the thumping like the boom of a drum beating louder, faster, rising to a crescendo, heralding a decision that ultimately he had no choice but to make.

He opened his arms to her and said simply, 'Come here.'

* * *

Briar collapsed into his arms, sobbing with relief, sobbing with happiness, and he kissed her tears away with the warmth of his lips, kissed her heartbreak away with one warm velvet mouth. She felt his tension radiating from his muscled flesh. She felt his need in the air they shared.

He lifted her into his arms and carried her through to the bedroom, undressing her slowly, reverentially, and shucking each garment away with a flick of his wrist while she scrabbled for his buttons and gave thanks to whatever force had shone over them and brought them back together.

And then, when they were both naked, he worshipped her body with his mouth, his hands and every part of him, travelling with her to that one blissful place that only they could share.

'Never leave me again,' he told her gruffly in the minutes afterwards while he stroked her hair as she lay nestled into him.

'I'm not planning on going anywhere,' she said.

'Now that would be a shame. I was about to suggest we might move this reconciliation to the shower.'

She smiled up at him. 'You have a real way with words, Mr Barrentes. Last one in is a rotten egg.'

He kissed her on her sassy mouth before she scooted out of the bed. He watched her go, enjoying the sway of her hips as she walked naked across the clothes littered floor, every lush curve of her, every movement a temptation to sin. *And he was just the man for the job.*

He was so glad she was back. He'd been mad to think he could ever live without her. He would never get enough of her. And he wanted more. So what was he still doing in bed? It was time to join her in the shower. And maybe time to give her the news that her father doing something active about his addiction was just what he'd been wanting to hear all along. It was good news and, if it were true, it was his intention to reintroduce funding, albeit with a few more controls in place from the start.

Briar washed her hands and splashed water on her face, catching sight of her reflection in the mirror. Were they really her eyes shining back at her? She looked so different already, just an hour after arriving, despite the persistent headache behind her eyes. But, even so, her skin was flushed, her eyes sparkling and her lips plump and pink.

She looked—*loved*. And why shouldn't she? She sure felt loved, whatever Diablo maintained about it not being on his agenda. Would she feel any better if he did profess to love her? Not likely.

She felt a familiar cramp down low, making more sense of the lingering headache, and placed a hand to her belly until the twinge eased. Soon she'd have her period and next month, when they made love, there'd be a chance she would give Diablo the baby he craved. Only this time it would be a baby both of them wanted.

Her fingers spread wide over her abdomen. Diablo's baby, growing inside her. How that prospect now seemed exciting where once she had been so fearful.

She reached down to the second drawer for a painkiller, only remembering that she'd cleared out her supplies when they'd left for the city. Had she brought any with her? She wrapped a towel around her, meeting Diablo on the way in. 'Leaving already?'

'I need my handbag,' she said. 'I think I left it in the car.'

'What's wrong?'

'Just some cramping. But I think I brought some pain relievers.'

He put his hands to her shoulders. 'Are you all right?'

'It's just my period coming. It's not serious.'

The moment she'd said the words she wanted to pull them right back. His mouth turned into a grim line. 'Your period.'

She touched his arm. 'Please don't be disappointed, Diablo. It's only the first month. It's no time at all. And it's not like we've been together every night. We have to have a better chance if we at least sleep together, right?'

He smiled. 'Of course, you're right. But be warned, next month I won't let you out of my sight.' He reached for his robe. 'I'll get it; you stay here.'

'I can do it,' she said, wishing she'd never said anything, but he was already gone.

She put a hand to her head as her headache kicked up a notch and a sick feeling fizzed dangerously in her gut.

The seconds turned into minutes but then he was back and handing over the bag along with a glass of water. Briar breathed a sigh of relief. So that was what had taken him so long.

'Th…thankyou,' she said, accepting the bag while moving a few steps away as nonchalantly as she could. 'Maybe you should get started in the shower?' she asked, wishing he would disappear.

'I can wait,' he said, his tone unreadable. She shivered as she unclipped the inner pocket and found her strip of pain relievers and was just removing them when that sick feeling in her stomach roiled again. *Because there was nothing else there.* She looked again. Not a thing. Yet there should have been the last couple of pills for this month and a brand-new strip besides—a strip she'd been intending to throw away. She frowned as she contemplated the painkillers in her hand.

'Something wrong?'

'No,' she said much too quickly while her mind did cartwheels trying to work out where she might have left them. At the apartment? At her parents' house?

'So you're not looking for these?'

She looked up, to see him brandishing the two damning strips, and felt her world slide away.

'I can explain…'

CHAPTER THIRTEEN

'DIABLO,' she pleaded, shaking her head as he waved the pills damningly in the air, 'it's not how it seems.'

'You're telling me you're not on the pill?'

'Yes! I mean no. I mean—'

'So you are on the pill.'

'Well, yes, but I was going off it—'

'Of course you were, which is why you have another packet, all ready to go. How many more do you have that you keep locked away somewhere else? Enough for six months? Twelve?'

'No, stop this. You have to listen to me.'

'Why the hell should I listen to you any longer? You've just promised me all kinds of love and devotion and life together, including professing a desire to be the mother of my children, and then I find you slipping a pill to ensure that never happens.'

'I wasn't! I wanted a painkiller for my headache—that's all. Nothing more than that.'

'You weren't going to take today's pill?'

She turned away and when she looked back she could see the executioner all ready to make the blow. 'I was just going to finish the course, that's all. Next month I wasn't going to take them. I'd already decided.'

He threw the strips rattling down on to the bed. 'No wonder

you didn't think you might be pregnant. No wonder you told me it was too early. All that time you were mocking me, because you knew there was no way you could be pregnant. It's *unlikely*, you said. "*It doesn't always happen*". But you were laughing behind my back. You had no intention of having my children.'

'It wasn't like that. You don't have any idea how guilty I've felt.'

'You've felt *nothing*! Not if you could break our agreement so coldly like that.'

'What agreement?'

'You know damned well—the one you signed when you agreed to become my wife. The one where you agreed to have my children.'

'Maybe I did sign it,' she slammed right back at him. 'I had no other choice if I was to try to save my family. But I never agreed to have your children. Because you never damned well asked me!'

'It was part of the contract!'

'Don't you think it was enough to expect me to marry you? How could you pin children on me as well? You knew I hated you then. What the hell were you thinking?'

'I was thinking you were *au fait* with the basic requirements of signing a contract and living with the conditions you'd agreed to with your signature. Obviously not. You had your own idea of what this marriage entailed.'

'Okay, so I objected to your assumption I'd have your children, but how else could I fight what I'd been corralled into? What do you think your mother would have thought about your plan to simply "produce" children?'

'What's my mother got to do with this?'

'Your mother was a woman who obviously loved deeply. You were the product of that love. Don't you think she'd be disappointed if she knew you wanted to create a child under contract, rather than it being the natural progression of a loving relationship?"

Silence, as heavy and dank as a storm cloud met her words.

'You don't know the first thing about my mother.'

'From what you've told me, I know she was a woman in love, a woman who loved her child because he was the product of that loving relationship, rather than because of what opportunities it might afford her in business.'

'And what's that got to do with you?'

She breathed out on a long sigh. 'You never gave me a chance. And yet I'm the one who came back today saying I want to make this marriage work. I'm the one who has decided to have your children, despite your heavy-handedness, because I want to, not because you've told me to.'

'Which is why you're on the pill, no doubt, because you're so keen to have those very children.'

She threw her hands up in the air. 'I don't believe you, Diablo. You should just listen to yourself some time. Maybe staying on the pill isn't such a bad idea after all. I'm not sure the world is ready for any more Diablos. One is no doubt more than enough.'

His eyes glistened, as slick and cold as black ice, his features darkening. 'Don't bother changing your practices on my account. Because it won't matter one iota. I was wrong to ever think you'd make a suitable mother for my children. I was wrong to ever think this could work.'

'Diablo,' she pleaded, suddenly aware of how close she was to losing him. She couldn't let that happen. She couldn't lose him again. 'But of course it can work. It will work—you'll see.'

'What I see,' he said, brushing her aside, 'is that it would have been better if you'd never come out here today.'

She reached out to him, crushed when he moved away in response. 'But I love you. You can't send me away. What do I have to do to prove I love you and want your children?'

He regarded her for a moment—so damningly that she knew she'd been judged and found wanting before he delivered his sentence. 'All I wanted was a wife who would bear my children. I never asked for her love. I never asked for it and I certainly never wanted it.'

Any hope she'd harboured for their future was snuffed out in his cold, analytical dismissal. She drew back.

'Then damn you, Diablo, you won't have either. At least not from me.'

She dragged on her clothes.

'So you're leaving me, once again?'

'I thought you were throwing me out,' she said, pulling on her boots. 'But don't worry, this time I won't be back.'

'So go,' he called after her. 'I won't stop you.'

She hurled herself from the house and left in a crunch of gears and a screech of tyres, cursing herself for her stupidity, cursing herself for deciding to finish the month's course rather than throw the damned pills away. She punched the wheel as the tears began to fall. 'No,' she protested, swiping at her eyes, not wanting to cry now, not when she needed to drive. But the tears became a deluge, flooding her vision, so instead of taking the turn for the highway, she turned down towards the town, finally pulling to a stop in the car park near the beach where she'd once shared coffee with Diablo.

Like the last time she'd been here, the beach was nearly deserted, the weekend visitors gone home. A walker strolled along the water's edge while a family group halfway between her and the water—a mother with three young sons—built a sand-castle to the enthusiastic encouragement of their yapping puppy.

She swallowed down on some ragged breaths and moved from the car's interior to the strip of lawn overlooking the beach. The sea breeze played with her hair and she turned her face into it, letting it cool her heated skin. She jammed her hands in her back pockets as she watched the matching pair of snowy-haired toddlers give up on building the sandcastle and run up and down the beach with the puppy instead, whooping into the wind as they threw a stick for the dog to fetch, their mother calling for them not to wander too far.

Diablo would have liked boys. And they would have been beautiful. Small, dark-haired boys with flashing dark eyes and long limbs. And an attitude. She smiled in spite of her grief. Oh, yes, *definitely* an attitude.

As sandcastles built by small children went, it was impressive, she could see, with turrets made out of upturned buckets of sand and the beginnings of a decent moat. One of the twins had returned to help dig and had bobbed down too close to his brother, with ensuing howls of protest and flailing of arms. Someone ended up with sand in his eyes and the howls intensified while their mother battled unsuccessfully to settle things down.

Briar smiled sadly and turned her attention to the sea once more. A movement caught her eye; something—a stick—flying low through the air, landing in the foaming wash. She sat up higher as the puppy bounded into the receding wash, eager to retrieve the prize for its young owner, even as the back wash carried the stick further out. The boy stood at the water's edge, calling for the puppy to come back, his little voice carried away by the wind as the dog paddled on, disappearing behind a wave.

Surely he wouldn't?

Already she was up on her feet, an uneasy feeling crawling through her bones even while she tried to tell herself not to panic. The walker had long ago disappeared into the distance, leaving the beach all but deserted. She watched as the boy turned and took a step towards his family, where the action and the shouts had escalated, before he obviously decided there was no help coming from that quarter and took off into an outgoing wave to rescue his puppy.

'No!' Briar yelled, wrenching off her boots and taking off across the beach, wishing she'd done something earlier. She should have alerted the mother, called out a warning—*anything*.

The mother looked up, surprised to see someone hurtling past even as she held her two fighting children apart.

'Your boy!' Briar called as she surged towards the shore, catching the mother's startled cry.

But the waves beat her, knocking the boy off his feet and spilling him into the water. She heard the mother scream behind her, spurring her on. She could still see the boy, his limbs flailing—she mustn't lose sight—before another wave crashed over him and he disappeared into the foaming water.

She scanned the water frantically where he'd disappeared, but the water was already pulling back and there was no sign of him. How could he vanish so quickly?

She raced through the shallows and plunged into the water, the icy temperature shorting her system, stunning her momentarily while she battled to get her bearings. Something scraped her arm—the puppy, the stick in its mouth, returning to shore. It was little consolation. Where was the boy? Already she could feel the undertow sucking at her, wanting to pull her down, wanting to fill her lungs with the sandy wash.

She dived under the next wave. If she went with the current, if she didn't try to fight it, she'd have more of a chance. She surfaced again, scanning the water around her, before ducking under, spinning around where the tossing tide let her, searching for a flash of colour, anything that would tell her where he was.

The rip had her again when she thought she saw it—the faintest hint of something light in the sand-tossed depths. Could it be the boy?

Her lungs bursting, she hit the surface, striking out, going where the current would take whatever it was she'd seen before she dived again, searching frantically for another glimpse of anything to give her hope. And then her hand brushed against something slippery—skin—and she grabbed hold as best she could and burst through the surface, gasping, dragging the boy's limp body with her.

Two things hit her simultaneously. Already they were metres out from shore, but, more critically, the boy didn't appear to be breathing. Already the adrenaline rush of diving into the water was seeping away, leaving her suddenly exhausted, his slack weight a heavy burden on her shoulder. How would she make it back to the beach in time for him—if she could make it back to the beach at all? But right now she had no choice. She had to try.

She cradled him under his chin, keeping him tucked close to her, and struck out towards the side of the bay where she knew the undertow wouldn't fight her so much, the muscles in her arms burning, the weight of water in her jeans a cold weight dragging her down.

Something churned the water nearby and her blood froze. Not sharks, not now! She tugged the boy closer, stroked harder despite her burning muscles.

'Briar!'

Diablo! She didn't know what he was doing there, but never had she been so happy to see anyone.

'The boy,' she gasped, still desperately stroking with her free arm while she battled to keep her face above the roll of the sea. 'He's not breathing. I don't know if I can make it.'

'*Dios*! I'll take him,' he said, relieving her of her precious burden. 'Can you make it by yourself?'

She nodded, already peeling off her jeans underwater and letting their unhelpful weight sink into the depths. 'Go,' she said, spitting out a mouthful of salt water. 'Get him to shore. I'll follow.'

'I'll be back,' he called, but already he was surging away. It was a struggle after that, but no longer the desperately urgent race to get to shore. She took her time, not trying to fight against the current, to eke out her energy. When she heard the roar of an outboard engine and saw the rubber dinghy heading towards her she knew she was saved.

'The boy?' she gasped as Diablo and a lifeguard dragged her on board and wrapped towels around her. 'How is he?'

'He'll make it. The paramedics revived him. He's on his way to hospital now.'

'Oh, thank God,' she said, giving in to the cold as violent shivers racked her body.

'You could have been killed,' Diablo told her, pulling her close to his side as the dinghy made for shore. 'I told you this beach had a bad rip.'

'Maybe you should have told the boy that!' She shivered again and pressed herself closer to his body, seeking his warmth despite his seething anger. Why should he be so angry? She knew she'd taken a risk but what choice had she had? The boy wouldn't have stood a chance otherwise. What was his problem?

'You should have called for the lifeguards.'

'There was no time! He would have drowned in a heartbeat.'

'*You* could have drowned in a heartbeat,' he said. 'You're lucky you survived.'

'I'm sorry I did, given all you seem to want is to tell me off.'

They hit the beach before he could respond and it seemed as if a dozen welcoming hands were waiting to haul her from the boat, which suited her just fine as her knees buckled beneath her. They carried her to a second ambulance waiting to check her out. A cuff was slapped on her arm and questions fired at her from all directions while Diablo stood brooding, drying himself off nearby.

A policeman took the details once the paramedics had finished their assessment. 'You're a lucky woman,' he told her, 'but that young Norton boy and his family have even more reason to be grateful. You saved his life. I'm sure the mother will want to thank you personally in a day or so.'

'We're both lucky my husband was there,' she admitted, nodding in Diablo's direction. 'I don't think I could have managed to bring him in on my own.'

The policeman closed his notebook. 'I was surprised to see Mr Barrantes in the water. It must have been difficult for him.'

She shook her head. 'I don't know what you mean.'

'You didn't know? His mother drowned on this beach five years ago. Two teenage girls got themselves into difficulties and she tried to help them. All three of them were swept out to sea. The girls washed up within a few days. It was three weeks before his mother's body was recovered.'

Ohmigod! She was vaguely aware of the policeman still talking but all her attention was now fixed on Diablo, standing with his hands on his hips, looking out over the choppy sea. He'd told her she'd died in a senseless accident. Now she understood. She'd drowned trying to save someone else's life. No wonder he'd chewed her out.

The policeman touched her gently on the shoulder. 'You should get warm. Are you going to the hospital for observation or have you decided to go home?'

She looked at the solitary figure of Diablo standing nearby. 'Home,' she said, though wondering where exactly that was now.

She stood up, testing her land legs. Why had Diablo been here? Was it purely coincidence he'd turned up at the beach when he had or had he followed her here? The barest glimmer of hope sparked inside her.

She walked to his side, still clutching the blanket tightly around her. 'Diablo?'

His eyes turned down towards hers although Briar had the distinct impression that he was still focusing on the sea.

'Diablo, thank you for what you did. I couldn't have managed without you.'

His mouth pulled tight as her words registered. She had brought his mother's death back, in unholy graphic horror. But the twisting in his gut right now wasn't entirely to do with re-membering what had happened back then. Something else was gnawing away at him, something else that had clamped a hold on his organs when he'd seen her running full pelt for the water and had driven him to follow her—the thought that he could lose her for ever when he'd only just recognised the truth himself.

He had to say something—anything—but this thing grabbing hold of his gut was squeezing down tight.

'I shouldn't have been so angry with you,' he managed at last. He tried to make it sound like an apology but his voice still came out gruff and disapproving. 'But what you did was still crazy.'

'I understand. And I'm sorry to do that to you. I only just heard how your mother died.' She touched his arm. 'But in that split second that child's life was the most important thing in the world. I'd watched him playing with his puppy. I'd seen how close he was to the water's edge and I'd done nothing. I could have alerted his mother, I could have done something. *I should have done something.* So, when I couldn't get to him fast enough, when I saw him sucked under those waves, I knew that if something happened to him I could never live with myself. But you saved us. You rescued both of us.'

He shook his head. '*You* saved the boy. I didn't even know there was a child in the water until I reached you. I thought…'

He raised a hand to his forehead. Oh, God, what he'd thought when he'd found her empty car and seen her plunging fully clothed into the waves! *Dios.* He hadn't stopped to think. He hadn't even registered that the woman screaming on the shore for help had been screaming for her own child. He'd thrown her his phone and told her to call emergency and he'd kicked off his shoes and dived in after Briar.

'You didn't realise there was a child?'

'No. I came after you.'

She must have sensed something in his voice; her lips were slightly parted, her amber eyes swirling with questions.

'Why were you at the beach?' she asked. 'How did you find me?'

'I watched you from the house. As soon as you'd cleared the gates I knew I'd made the biggest mistake of my life. I hadn't listened to you. I'd never given you a chance. I knew without a shadow of a doubt that this time you wouldn't come back—and I had to get you back. When I saw your car take the road into the town I knew I had a chance to catch you.'

Her lips turned into a tremulous smile. 'You came after me.'

He reached down and took her hands in his. 'I couldn't believe I'd been stupid enough to let you go again. So when I saw you diving into that surf I knew I had to find you so I could tell you…'

'Tell me what?' she whispered.

He sighed. 'This isn't easy for me to say, but when I watched you drive away back then it felt like my heart ripped in two.'

Her eyes shone up at him, bright and uncertain.

'I love you, Briar. I had to follow you and let you know. There was no way I was not going to find you in that water. There was no way I was going to lose you again.'

'You love me?' she questioned. 'You always said—'

'I know what I said. I was wrong.'

'I don't believe it,' she cried, tears filling her eyes. 'You love me. You really love me. And you're never going to lose me.'

'I thought I already had,' he told her. 'When I took you so savagely on our wedding night and you cried and ran from the bed. Already I feared I'd lost you.'

His words revealed another side of him she'd never suspected. 'But I wasn't crying because of what you'd—we'd—done. Don't you know, I was crying because you'd broken through my defences so completely? I wanted you, even when I told myself I shouldn't.'

'I didn't hurt you?'

'I loved what you did to me, the way you moved, the way you made me feel when you made love to me. I'd never felt so alive and that's what scared me so much. That's why I cried.' She raised a hand to his face, her eyes widening. 'So is that why you didn't want to make love to me after that?'

He clasped her hand, brought it to his mouth and kissed it. 'Oh, I did. Believe me. But I knew I'd been so rough with you—too rough. I wanted you to have time to recover and to find you did want to make love with me. But I couldn't believe it when you took so long.'

She laughed, remembering. 'You certainly didn't make it easy for me.' Her smile widened. 'I love you so much, Diablo.'

'And I love you.' His lips dipped lower, sweeping over hers in the gentlest of passes that promised so much more. 'But tell me—there's something I must know.'

Her eyes moved from his lips to his eyes, a tiny frown creasing her brow. 'What's that?'

'It occurs to me that in our arrangements before I omitted to ask you something important.' He suddenly dropped to one knee before her. 'Briar, will you marry me?'

She beamed down at him, salt water once again filling her eyes, only this time it was tears. 'Oh, Diablo, I'd say yes in a heartbeat. You know that. But I can't, I'm already married.'

He looked up at her amber eyes and her lush mouth, already mentally preparing for his next assault on that and all points south just as soon as he got her home.

'Then do you promise to stay married, forgoing all others, and to share your husband's home and his future and his love, for ever and ever?'

She cocked her head suspiciously. 'I'm assuming there's no obeying involved in this arrangement?'

He gave a low chuckle that hummed right through her. 'Mr Barrentes wouldn't be so foolish as to ask.'

'In that case,' she told him, pulling him up and wrapping her arms around his neck, 'I do.'

And then Diablo kissed his bride.

EPILOGUE

Twelve months later

THEY arrived two weeks early in a flurry of excitement—two dark-haired babies, one brandishing the flashing dark eyes of his father, the other with the misty blue that would make way to a lighter colour over time.

Now, barely twenty-four hours later in their private hospital suite, Diablo watched as they lay supported on pillows, suckling at their mother's breasts.

'*Dios*,' he said, cupping each baby's soft downy head in the palm of his hand, 'I have never seen anything more beautiful. You have made me the happiest man in the world.'

Briar beamed up at him. 'Aren't they both perfect?'

'It is no wonder,' he said, pressing his lips to her forehead, 'when they have such a perfect mother. You were magnificent during the birth. I wanted to at once weep with joy and yet cry at the pain you were going through. I have never before felt so helpless.'

'Thank you,' she said, 'for just being there and squeezing my hand.'

Diablo helped her ease the sleepy babies into a burp and then into their cribs beside the bed.

'And now all we need for them are the perfect names,' she

said. 'Have you thought any more about naming them after your parents?'

'Cosmo and Camilla?' He smiled. 'I like it very much. Our boy should be Cosmo Nathaniel, don't you think?'

'Oh, Diablo,' she said over the lump in her throat, one hand over her mouth while the other reached for her husband's. 'To name him after my brother, it would mean so much to my parents—to all of us.'

He nodded. 'I know. And if it was, as the counsellors believe, your brother's death that drove your father to the desperation that led to his gambling, then maybe this child can help keep him well. Cosmo Nathaniel Barrentes it is. And, as for Camilla…' He reached over and touched the pads of his fingers to the soft newborn down of her temples. 'Her name should be Amber. Amber Camilla.' He turned to his wife. 'Do you like it?'

'I do. But I don't understand. Why Amber?'

He moved his hand from his child's temple to his wife's. 'The answer is here, in the colour of your eyes. I love how the colour changes and throws sparks when you are angry, or shines like gold when you are happy, like you are now, or turns molten when we make love. I want to name our child after your beautiful eyes—the eyes of the woman I love.'

He tipped up her chin with his fingers. 'And I *do* love you, Briar, with all my heart and soul.'

And the man she loved kissed her so tenderly, so sweetly, that she could feel his love reaching out, enveloping her in its thick, warm folds, and she smiled to herself as he deepened the kiss. Her husband might never have believed in fairy tales, but she knew their happy ever after was only just beginning.

BILLI◉NAIRES' BRIDES

Pregnant by their princes...

Take three incredibly wealthy European princes
and match them with three beautiful, spirited women.
Add large helpings of intense emotion and passionate
attraction. Result: three unexpected pregnancies...and
three possible princesses—if those princes have their way.

THE ITALIAN PRINCE'S PREGNANT BRIDE
by Sandra Marton

It was payday for international tycoon Prince Nicolo Barbieri.
But he wasn't expecting what would come with his
latest acquisition: Aimee Black—who, it seemed,
was pregnant with Nicolo's baby!

Available in August.

Also available from this miniseries;

THE GREEK PRINCE'S CHOSEN WIFE
September

THE SPANISH PRINCE'S VIRGIN BRIDE
October

REQUEST YOUR FREE BOOKS!

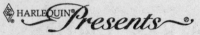 

2 FREE NOVELS
PLUS 2
FREE GIFTS!

PASSION GUARANTEED SEDUCTION

YES! Please send me 2 FREE Harlequin Presents® novels and my 2 FREE gifts. After receiving them, if I don't wish to receive any more books, I can return the shipping statement marked "cancel." If I don't cancel, I will receive 6 brand-new novels every month and be billed just $3.80 per book in the U.S., or $4.47 per book in Canada, plus 25¢ shipping and handling per book and applicable taxes, if any*. That's a savings of close to 15% off the cover price! I understand that accepting the 2 free books and gifts places me under no obligation to buy anything. I can always return a shipment and cancel at any time. Even if I never buy another book from Harlequin, the two free books and gifts are mine to keep forever.

106 HDN EEXK 306 HDN EEXV

Name   (PLEASE PRINT)

Address   Apt. #

City   State/Prov.   Zip/Postal Code

Signature (if under 18, a parent or guardian must sign)

Mail to the **Harlequin Reader Service®**:
IN U.S.A.: P.O. Box 1867, Buffalo, NY 14240-1867
IN CANADA: P.O. Box 609, Fort Erie, Ontario L2A 5X3

Not valid to current Harlequin Presents subscribers.

Want to try two free books from another line?
Call 1-800-873-8635 or visit www.morefreebooks.com.

* Terms and prices subject to change without notice. NY residents add applicable sales tax. Canadian residents will be charged applicable provincial taxes and GST. This offer is limited to one order per household. All orders subject to approval. Credit or debit balances in a customer's account(s) may be offset by any other outstanding balance owed by or to the customer. Please allow 4 to 6 weeks for delivery.

Your Privacy: Harlequin is committed to protecting your privacy. Our Privacy Policy is available online at www.eHarlequin.com or upon request from the Reader Service. From time to time we make our lists of customers available to reputable firms who may have a product or service of interest to you. If you would prefer we not share your name and address, please check here. ☐

HP07

HARLEQUIN®

Mediterranean NIGHTS™

Glamour, elegance, mystery and revenge aboard the high seas...

Coming in August 2007...

THE TYCOON'S SON

by
award-winning author

Cindy Kirk

Businessman Theo Catomeris's long-estranged father is determined to reconnect with his son, so he hires Trish Melrose to persuade Theo to renew his contract with Liberty Line. Sailing aboard the luxurious *Alexandra's Dream* is a rare opportunity for the single mom to mix business and pleasure. But an undeniable attraction between Trish and Theo is distracting her from the task at hand....

Always passionate, always proud.

The richest royal family in the world— a family united by blood and passion, torn apart by deceit and desire.

By royal decree, Harlequin Presents is delighted to bring you *The Royal House of Niroli*. Step into the glamorous, enticing world of the Nirolian Royal Family. As the king ails, he must find an heir…each month an exciting new installment follows the epic search for the true Nirolian king. Eight heirs, eight romances, eight fantastic stories!

Be sure not to miss any of the passion!

Coming in August:

SURGEON PRINCE, ORDINARY WIFE

by Melanie Milburne

When brilliant surgeon Dr. Alex Hunter discovers he's the missing Prince of Niroli long thought dead, he is torn between duty and his passion for Amelia Vialli, who can never be his queen….

Coming in September:

BOUGHT BY THE BILLIONAIRE PRINCE
by Carol Marinelli

HARLEQUIN *Presents*

Surrender To The Sheikh

**He's proud, passionate, primal—
dare she surrender to the sheikh?**

Feel warm winds blowing through your hair and the
hot desert sun on your skin as you are transported to
exotic lands. As the temperature rises, let yourself be
seduced by our sexy, irresistible sheikhs.

If you love our men of the desert, look for more stories
in this enthralling miniseries coming soon!

Rosalie Winters doesn't engage in the games of flirtation
that Sheikh Arik expects from women—but once
Rosalie is under his command, she'll open up to receive
the loving that only he can give her.

FOR THE SHEIKH'S PLEASURE

by Annie West